TH

NEνν

SEASON

THE HILARIOUS ESCAPADES
OF UNCONVENTIONAL
NOT SO INNOCENT
VILLAGE LIFE

AND THOSE WHO LIVE IN IT!

JENNER PUBLICATIONS
Inspiration from Suffolk

OTHER TITLES AVAILABLE INCLUDE

PUBLISHED

Apr 2004	THE BOWLS CLUB
Nov 2005	THE NEW SEASON
Nov 2007	GOING INDOORS

FORTHCOMING

TANTRUMS ON TOUR
SNUGGLETUM

THE POET'S COLLECTION

LOVE AND REFLECTION
THE MODERN WORLD
SADNESS AND SORROW
WAR AND PEACE
INSPIRED THOUGHT

THE
NEW
SEASON

JENNER PUBLICATIONS
Inspiration from Suffolk

THE NEW SEASON
Paul Hammond
Second Edition

First Published November 2005
Reprinted November 2008

Published by Jenner Publications
C/o Wild About Birds
Main Road, Theberton, Suffolk IP16 4RA
www.jennerpublications.co.uk

ISBN Number 978-0954663315

Distributed by Jenner Publications

Printed in England by Barnwell Print Ltd
Dunkirk, Aylsham, Norfolk NR11 6SU

Illustrations © Sonya E Burrows

Katrina, Elliot and Jamie

This is for you

INTRODUCTION

I n the sleepy countryside of Suffolk, amid the ancient willows and thatched cottages of peaceful hamlets lies the small village of Lower South-Borough.

Surrounded by picturesque duck pond, heraldic sign, carefully trimmed hedgerows and freshly swept pathways, there stands a tired wooden building with an objective lean (depending on the wind direction).

Nearby, a small pile of bricks under an old tarpaulin promises possibilities of potential new construction, as they have done for many a year. Weathered timber seats stand proudly in front of a more robust timber framework.

This is the members' 'clubhouse', a Victorian structure whose majestic windows offer, when cleaned, a splendid panoramic inspection of the on-goings outside. The clubhouse overlooks a magnificent lawn, rectangular in shape, which on closer inspection proves to have a formidable ditch and bank much like a medieval castle but with numbers and markers attached to its structure.

The grass is short, mostly, with some threadbare patches towards its edges, but its carefully manicured form leaves the visitor in no doubt that this is indeed the village bowling green.

May beckons with a hint of summer in the air as the warm sun rises over the trees. Birds begin to sing, butterflies flutter and the distant 'putt-putt' of a small two-stroke engine disturbs the distant tranquil calm.

It is the warming motor of the club's ancient lawnmower emerging from a ramshackle, recently stained shed at the edge of the green, announcing to all that it is indeed the first day of the new bowling season. The Revd Percival Peabody proudly prepares for the new day ahead, his first in the honorary position as 'assistant keeper', more importantly his first solo venture in 'green preparation'.

So welcome then to the new day, the first day of another season with the members, family, friends and associates of Lower South-Borough Bowling Club. Now, for the first time, meet the characters face to face as they gather again for the new season.

Experience the thrill of club competition, the cut and thrust of the tearoom at lunch time and the sheer brilliance of skilled uproarious debate at social gatherings.

From the very first day, the summer builds through triumph and disaster, lurching from adventure holidays to county competitions, from friendly practice sessions to royal visits, and from unbelievable catalogues of coincidences that snatch defeat from the jaws of victory.

There's no denying the fact that in the world of Lower South-Borough here lies a club with some extra-ordinary men and women, and perhaps even one or two bowlers. Then of course there's always the day to day calamities of village life itself to keep Percy on his toes, or sometimes his knees!

If the onset of another new season isn't bad enough, the appearance of Rollo, the rather 'disturbed' vicarage cat, is bound to create anarchy at every opportunity. His short temper, sharp claws and unwitting dislike for anything 'bowling' serve only to systematically reduce even the best laid plans to complete chaos.

ADVENTURE WEEKENDS, MANIACAL LAWNMOWERS,
BROKEN BOWLS, MISSING COACHES, WRONG DATES,
SPLIT TROUSERS, MEN IN SKIRTS,
SUSPECT STICKERS, CRAZED CLERGY,
INEBRIATED SALESMEN, TEA COSIES,
ARACHNOPHOBIC TEA LADIES,
STALE HAM SANDWICHES.

And so much more as the club live up to its motto....

'WHATEVER CAN GO WRONG, PROBABLY WILL'

All characters, places, and definitions within this book are fictional,
although some readers may feel a familiarity and empathy with
some characterisation.

ACKNOWLEDGEMENTS

I 'd like to express my deeply appreciation to the every bowler worldwide for their support and inspiration. Thank you also to all the team at POTTERS LEISURE, for always giving my books such a tremendous launch every year.

Special thanks to all the long-suffering members of SOLE BAY and HALESWORTH ANGEL Bowls Clubs, I hope you enjoy the challenge of trying to work out who's in the book. Who knows, there might just be one or two members from other clubs too?

Thanks to Dennis Driver and Jack Woods for some challenging moments and enjoyable memories from Britannia.

Thanks also to all my family, especially to my wonderful Mum who's always been so supportive; my dear departed Dad - I wish you were here to see this; also to my long suffering and very special brother Roger. A very big hello to Charlotte and Michael for the inspiration for the two children's parts.

Well done Colin for being inspirational in portraying the unintentional but well matched Percival Peabody, our very own vicar.

To Pickles, our madcap, manic, and crazy cat I have to say you were so right to play the part of Rollo. Also thanks to the very patient and talented artist Sonya for creating the caricatures for this edition.

A very large compliment to John Walford, legendary for his dinner table jokes, for being the source of so much humour.

It's been a lot of fun writing this and a lot of the stories are very much based on real life events. I hope you all enjoy the book and of course there's always the fear of several follow up manuscripts.

Best wishes

Paul Hammond

CONTENTS

5. AUGUST   THE FESTIVAL OF BOWLS

The club's big day until the guests arrive, 'Sticky' comes unstuck in the finals, the salesman gets led astray, and all in all it's a close run thing. 'Big Jim' loses his dignity, Squiffy loses his trousers but wins the day, issues get heated over stickers, Tony cleans up, Rollo gets retribution and Molly finds love.

6. EPILOGUE

Percy closes the green in style.

MEET THE MEMBERS

The Men

HON. PRESIDENT   Ronald 'Squiffy' Regis
Former RAF Squadron Commander still living in 1942, bowls like a Barnes Wallis bouncing bomb. Now the retired club president.

CHAIRMAN   Bernard 'Batty' Bartrum
Dubious DIY plumber, definitely a ladies' man, always in a pickle, very inquisitive, talkative and sometimes acts a bit too rashly.

VICE CHAIRMAN   Douglas Doolittle MBE
Retired surgeon, a posh and wealthy suburbanite, one of those 'fair play' guys who guarantees a good game and never cheats.

HON. SECRETARY   Charles 'Charlie' Chesterford
Former cricketer, couldn't play, nothing has changed! He likes a tipple, is a bit of a practical joker and loves money making scams.

HON. TREASURER   Reginald Trimley Esq.
Accountant, short-sighted, well meaning but easily flustered, fairly naïve in all things non-accountable, but hot on figures.

HON. COMP. SEC.   Jack 'Big Jim' Tuttle
One-time county legend, larger than life, eats for England, drinks like a fish, a funny comedian, everyone's favourite speech maker!

HON. TOURING TEAM SEC.   (Position vacant)
Life beyond Suffolk has never been discovered.

CAPTAIN   Rt. Hon. Clifford James Johnson
A traditional working class councillor, well-respected and a good bowler, but still very much 'Jack the Lad' with looks to match.

VICE CAPTAIN   Derek Dunstable
Quick tempered, average bowler, a fiery combination, always
argumentative and never ever wrong, advisable to run for cover!

GREEN KEEPER   Patrick 'Postie' Albright
Retired postman, very keen and serious, a 'by the book' player who
loves his green more than life itself, don't upset him!

ASSISTANT GREEN KEEPER   Revd Percival 'Percy' Peabody
Very helpful, eager, accident prone, single, sincere cat owner who
can't bowl but can paint, is well meaning, loveable and innocent.

CLUB CHAMPION   Dennis 'Sticky' Ditherford
Excellent bowler, tall, slightly built, prone to talking too much, has
a real tendency to fake injury. A keen 'twitcher' and a dramatist.

TOURNAMENT UMPIRE   Eric 'Chalkie' Tunstall
Retired pilot, enjoys life, plays a jolly good game, now slightly
detached and never really left the war but still game for anything!

THE BARMAN   Bertie Tattleford
Double glazing sales rep., explosive, cocky, bowls well at times, an
exuberant individual, well meaning at heart; a naturalist too!

COACH   Tony 'Trigger' Havershall
Council worker, serious player, all round nice guy but easily distracted
and not too clever. Has some very unusual, questionable hobbies.

CLUB MEMBER   David Dimpley
Retired, humorous, easy going, brilliant bowler when awake.

CLUB MEMBER   Colin Spindleforth
Thirty-something family man with a mid-life crisis in everything.

CLUB MEMBER   Russell Cobblethwaite
Long serving, most senior member, 70 years young, still sharp.

CLUB MEMBER   Frenchie 'Wide Boy' Phillips
Silver tongued, fast talking ladies' man, always on the move.

CLUB MEMBER   James 'Scottie' McCarver
Talks a good game, but easily distracted, loves his whisky.

CLUB MEMBER   Paul Jenner
Upcoming new kid on the block, very competitive, still learning.

CLUB MEMBER   Johnny Jackson
Club's hottest signing, an aspiring county and national player.

NEW ARRIVAL   Olly 'Ever Ready' Ramsbottom
Full of dodgy ideas, a definite 'wide boy' with the gift of the gab.

JUNIOR MEMBER   Timothy 'Tiny' Doolittle
The son, now 14 years old always eager to play and to play up!

SELECTION COMMITTEE
Who ever is available and foolish enough to volunteer.

The Ladies

CAPTAIN   Doris 'Posh' Doolittle
Impoverished socialite, vegan, questionable high morals with a liking for a tipple or two. A devout defender of womens' bowling.

CLUB CHAMPION   Sheila 'Legs' Ramsbottom
Aussie girl, cocky, sharp, definitely a match for any man around the bar and at the card table! A feisty handful on and off the green.

COMP. SEC.   Diane Ditherford
Long-suffering wife, gossips for England, unorthodox bowler with a voice that would cut glass. Has a tendency to get things mixed up.

COMMITTEE REP.　　　　　　　　Cynthia Cobblethwaite
Forthright, warm-hearted, popular all rounder, nice lady, does a lot
of charity work, but naïve with it. Still fights for her beliefs though!

PRESIDENT (ELECT)　　　　　　Gloria 'Smiler' Grimshaw
Never a dull moment or a happy one, renowned for steel britches,
lack of humour and stentorian personality; definately a cold fish!

CLUB MEMBER　　　　　　　　　Pauline Jenner
Wannabe mum, highly ambitious, somewhat blunt.

CLUB MEMBER　　　　　　　　　Molly Coddle
Long-suffering tea lady and long term spinster.

CLUB MEMBER　　　　　　Phillippa Spindleforth
Working class councillor aspiring to be posh, but a culinary geinius!

NEW ARRIVAL　　　　　　　　Sarah Jane Coddle
Former black sheep of the Coddle family, saucy, sensuous, sultry,
seductive and suggestive, apparently a real man eater?

JUNIOR MEMBER　　　　　Abbey 'Spice' Doolittle
The daughter, 12 years old, going on 22 and a wannabe model.

and then there was...

ROLLO
Disturbed, long haired, maniacal, mischievous, mayhem causing,
madcap, short-tempered, scheming and misbehaving vicarage cat!

MISS MATILDA BAGSHOTT (Baggie)
Gloria's posh Persian pussy, long of hair, short on temper, never
preened, supposedly snobbish and a bit of a tart as well as a cat.

REVEREND ARCHIBALD (Archie)
A bull dog with a big attitude to compensate for his bow legs, cross-
eyed expression, drooling mouth and inbuilt hate of cats.

THE PARISH COMMUNITY

The Rt Hon. E. A. Thomas the 3rd	**Bishop**
The Rt Hon. M. J. Twiggle	**Archbishop**
Dr Boris Binder-Garden	**Vet**
Harry 'The Hammer' Huckstable	**Organist**
Peter 'Chippie' Barryman	**Recycling manager**
Reverend Joshua Jackson	**Percy's predecessor**
Jiggy 'Snapper' Jenkins	**Paparazzi hotshot**
Jimmy 'Monkey' Murphy	**Builder**
Johnny 'Midge' McPherson	**Builder**
Godfrey Go-Lightly	**County vice-president**
Martin King	**National champion**
Tony 'Tick Tock' Ballcock	**National president**
The Rt. Hon. Lady Quinton MBE	**Ladies president (ret.)**
James 'Jamie' Gotthelott	**Store proprietor**
Sam 'Iron Man' Harris	**County president**

Mrs Jones	**Local parishioner**
Sir John 'Jeremiah' Tinkleton	**Touring president**
Matilda Elizabeth Tinkleton	**Touring captain**
Tim	**Valley Tours driver**
Joshua	**Adventure World Rep.**
'Boom Boom' Baker DSO MBE	**Retired air marshall**
Sgt Major Sid 'Snotty' Snodgrass	**Territorial Army**
Joe 'Dodger' Stubbs	**F. H. Promotions**
Johnny 'Greaser' Stubbs	**F.H. Holiday Tours**
Little Jimmy Blodger	**School bully**
David Van Stem	**TOTTERS manager**
Manuelle 'Burrito' Mondago	**TOTTERS head chef**
Dazzling Bluecoats	**TOTTERS stewards**

Even as we speak the parish of Lower South-Borough continues to flourish and grow…

CHAPTER ONE

APRIL
PREPARATIONS

'It was no good, no good at all,' he muttered under his breath.

The Revd Percival Peabody was having a bad day and it was, after all, only 6.30 in the morning.

The butter hadn't even melted yet on his freshly toasted slice of Mrs Spindleforth's newly baked Sunday batch.

He looked out of the window again in abject disgust as the rain continued to do what it always did best...

It wasn't really rain at all, more like monsoon season in Calcutta, only worse. In fact Revd Peabody was quite sure that it would be possible to re-enact the 'parting of the Red Sea' on his front lawn.

At least he supposed he still had a front lawn underneath all that water.

The goldfish in his pond didn't seem to mind at all.

Now that it was brim full to overflowing they were swimming round his back garden quite merrily.

Sadly the worms were not so happy.

Aqualungs for worms had not yet been invented, and those that had managed to survive so far were being avidly pursued across the wet rockery garden by an increasingly excited blackbird with six babies in tow.

The freshly washed bowling greys had seemed fine the evening before, drying in the early summer breeze.

It wasn't really the Reverend's fault that they had been left on the line all night; it was merely a case of him being slightly forgetful.

Many was the time he poured himself a freshly brewed cup of tea to start the day anew, only to discover, by means of the rapidly growing wet patch on his leg, that the teacup was still upside down in its saucer.

His only consolation was perhaps that he had forgotten to switch on the kettle in the first place, so the water was still icy cold and unrelenting.

'Things are not getting off to a good start,' he muttered, and, today of all days, he really did need a watchful eye from the Lord and not too many '*Hail Marys*'.

He picked up the slightly saturated daily newspaper from the equally saturated doormat and decided that perhaps it would be better to read it later.

With that in mind, he deposited the offending article over the nearby radiator.

He glanced over to the calendar by the kitchen door, and the ink-written, larger than life, reminder stared back with equal boldness from the date…

April 30th…

The day before the new outdoor bowling season!

It was Reverend Peabody's first day at the club in his role as 'newly promoted' assistant green keeper.

Only the previous evening the phone had rung at an uncommonly late hour just after the Reverend had 'retired' for the night.

After much panic and mayhem, which included tripping over Rollo, the equally rotund vicarage cat, the Reverend had arrived in a riotous tumble at the bottom of the stairs amid bedclothes, cat food and freshly ironed linen.

Rollo was not impressed; his tail was firmly wedged under the Reverend's rather imposing bottom.

The phone continued to ring, which perhaps wasn't the best of things to happen, perched as it was, rather precariously on Reverend Peabody's throbbing and rather battered head.

Percy reached for the phone cautiously, eager to escape its shrill vibrating overtones yet not wishing to incur further injury from its falling handset.

Rollo however had other ideas, pinned as he was, very painfully, to the shag pile by the Reverend's large posterior.

With an ear splitting yowl Rollo planted his fully extended claws firmly in the impressionable fleshy weight.

It was mentioned in the village later that the Reverend's equally resounding cry of protest dislodged seven tiles from the church roof and cleared Mrs Jones' constipation instantaneously.

Rollo disappeared with great gusto out of the front door cat flap leaving it banging back and forth much like the sound of a demented woodpecker.

At the bottom of the stairs the Reverend still lay, amid the clothing chaos, one hand nursing his head, the other massaging his equally painful posterior.

'Hello.'

Percival Peabody looked around.

'Hello, are you there Percy?'

The voice appeared to be coming from his freshly ironed underwear now lying on the third step of the staircase.

Percival stared at the Y-fronts bemusedly; he was not sure that the Good Book covered conversations with demonically possessed underwear.

The underwear moaned again.

'Percy, pick up the phone and stop playing around!'

Realisation sank in.

Easing his damaged bottom onto a pile of soft towels Reverend Percival Peabody sighed a deep sigh of relief and extracted the phone from the Y-fronts.

'Hello, Percy here…' said Percival, offering the blatantly obvious to the harassed caller.

'Percy… it's Patrick… Patrick Albright.'

There was a slight pause and then the phone continued its conversation.

'Now listen Percy, I've had a bit of a breakdown in the car and can't get to the clubhouse. You'll have to go in instead and prepare the grass for the start of the season tomorrow'

The Reverend stared into the phone with a mixture of fear, trepidation and boyish awareness; he began to protest weakly...

'But…But…But...'

'No buts, Percy. You should know how to use the mower and the keys are hanging up by the front door of the shed.'

'But...'

C-L-A-N-G!

The phone went dead as the handset was firmly replaced at the other end.

Percy stared at the now useless receiver in his hand and reflected on the conversation just past.

Well, it was no surprise that Patrick's car had broken down, really, was it?

After all it was made in the sixties and hadn't seen a new spark plug in 15 years...

Whilst Patrick had often delighted in taking his family and friends down to the sea to try out his new surfboard it hadn't really helped the car when the tide came in whilst Patrick was out.

Realisation dawned suddenly...

THE LAWN-MOWER!

Percy shivered nervously as his memory conjured a rather bleak dark picture of the ancient machine lying in the depths of the Lower South-Borough Bowling Club tool shed.

No one in their right mind would ever call it a lawn-mower, unless 'Postie' was in earshot.

Patrick 'Postie' Albright was infatuated by his range of pre-Victorian hardware with which he lovingly cared for the club green.

The 'lawn-mower' no longer possessed any paint, or in fact anything resembling décor. It was a complex mass of metal blades, nuts, bolts and springs buried in a deep mulch of oil and thick grease.

There were indentations along the heavily reinforced 'cuttings box' where unfortunate woods had collided *en route* to the waiting cot.

Percival had naturally assumed that he would have a number of seasons to acquire the full repertoire of Patrick's vast knowledge.

He was all too aware that a minimum of a master's degree in quantum physics was required to understand the principles of using 'The Beast of South-Borough'.

Percival sighed the sort of sigh one usually associates with a rapidly deflating beach ball, and potted his underpants deftly into the offensive Chinese vase in the corner.

It really hadn't been a good end to the day.

Percy shook his head and focused on the events in hand, bringing him back to the reality of the present day.

* * * *

Two hours later a rather bedraggled, befuddled and slightly dampened Percival Peabody arrived in all his humble splendour at the gates to the club bowling green.

He had been doing quite well: despite the persistent downpour, he had steered his loyal but rather rusty cycle along the potted and pitted lane managing to miss the more threatening or deep-looking puddles.

In fact there were one or two he was sure were mine shafts cunningly disguised as puddles, down which he could have disappeared, never to be found...

He had intended to arrive at the club in a fairly dry condition with nothing more than an enterprising trickle or two managing to gain access to his gaping neckline.

And so, he had very nearly made it to the club gate intact when nature and fate took a fickle turn in the Reverend's rapidly deteriorating day.

He had absolutely no idea at all that Rollo, the rectory cat, with a now somewhat flatter tail, had sought refuge nearby to console himself and his ruffled fur.

In fact, he was a lot closer than Percival could possibly imagine.

So close in fact, he was at that very moment curled up under the slightly ajar waterproof covering that adorned the tired wicker basket on the front of the Reverend's bicycle.

Having inspected his squashed appendage for signs of permanent damage Rollo had finally settled down to indulge in a pastime that only cats can indulge in best at 9.00 in the morning, that of sleeping...

His head dropped into his lap, his kinked tail settled in a more or less straight line and then curled around the deep shag pile that resembled his coat.

BUMP!

His left eye opened warily...

BUMP!

His right eye joined it in a somewhat alarmed state...

BUMP! BUMP! BUMP!

Rollo bounced around the basket much like an out-of-control hovercraft, his hackles rising, as the front wheel circumnavigated the potholes.

BUMP! BUMP!

SPLASH!

Enough was enough, and it is a well known fact that cats and water are not a good combination at the best of times.

The deep scarring on the linoleum floor in the bathroom already bore witness to the many bath-time struggles between Rollo and the Reverend's house-keeper attempting to give the cat 'a bit of a spruce up'.

Percy had no idea what was to ensue as his front wheel dipped into the offending puddle at great speed.

The water rose in equal arcs either side of the wheel, soaking the wicker basket with a fair mixture of rainwater, mud and gravel.

Rollo emerged from the basket in a giant ball of wet fur, limp tail and outstretched claws, spitting, snarling and complaining loudly as he almost reached escape velocity in three seconds flat.

Percy, having no warning whatsoever, did what anyone else would have logically done…

He screamed very loudly and let go of the handlebars, his only concern being to protect his tender extremities from the whirling dervish that had suddenly materialised from nowhere.

Things became somewhat muddled and confused after that…

The cat impacted with the Reverend's nose, the front wheel impacted with a large hole and came to an abrupt and immediate halt, and the Reverend, with cat attached, sailed with great gusto over the offending handlebars.

SPLASH!

Percival landed almost with perfection, dead centre in the largest deepest puddle he had ever known.

Settling rather quickly up to his waist in the muddy water he bore witness to an equally wet cat decimating the hedgerow plants in a maniacal fit of bad temper and mutually assured disaster…

One should really never pick a fight with a dense patch of stinging nettles!

He would probably have had time to find it mildly amusing, had the bike not arrived at the exact same spot in the puddle and deposited itself, seat, basket and handlebar, squarely in his ample stomach.

The cat disappeared through the hedgerow at great speed with much noise, closely followed by the flying bicycle as Percival finally gave vent to his frustrations in a physical display of temper tantrums.

He extracted himself gingerly from the puddle and, clutching his now tender midriff, turned towards the club gate.

'Morning Reverend.'

The Rt Hon. Ronald 'Squiffy' Regis stood by the gate, padlock and key in hand, looking on at the débâcle with a somewhat amused smile breaking beneath his handlebar moustache.

'Trifle inclement, what?' he spouted.

Percy groaned. It really was a bad start to the season and it couldn't get any worse, could it?

It most certainly could…

* * * *

The steam rose from the Reverend's drying clothes, laid out across the rather splendid hearth of Squiffy's antique fireplace.

As he clutched the freshly brewed cup of hot sweet tea in his frozen hands Percival reflected on his stroke of luck that the club president lived next door to the bowling green.

His nose began to glow warmly from the effects of the warm fire and perhaps also the spot or two of brandy that Squiffy was known to pop into every pot.

Many a lady of good repute was known to have been seen staggering from his front door on a warm summer afternoon having sampled the delights of his country cream teas.

Rumour had it that the very stern and somewhat snobbish Phillippa Spindleforth had sampled a touch too much of his good hospitality, taken the wrong turn in the dark and finished up 'going to bed' in the clubhouse cloakroom (much to the delight of the visiting county president's team the following morning).

Phillippa of course vehemently denied any such stories, simply stating that she had been 'cleaning out the cloakroom' and had got stuck under the pile of lost jackets.

Percival stared out of the window at his now rather battered vicarage bicycle. The handlebars were rather askew, looking more like a pair of cow's horns, whilst the front wheel resembled a rollercoaster ride.

He wondered briefly if it would pass as a modern art sculpture for which he could obtain a small grant.

'Here you are, Percy!'

Percival turned round as the jolly face of the club president appeared in the doorway, his extended left arm decked with a spare pair of jeans and woolly jumper.

Percy mumbled his gratitude and, taking the offerings, turned back to the warmth of the fire where his drying trousers now blazed merrily like a miniature campfire.

'Oh my God!' stuttered Percy.

'Ha! Ha!' chortled Squiffy, 'that's torn it; you're in the hot seat now!'

Squiffy chuckled gleefully, somewhat amused at his own wisecrack.

'I always said you were stuck in the seventies, old chap, well you've got yourself a pair of flares now!'

He sniggered very loudly...

'More like hot pants!' gurgled Squiffy

'Hee hee hee!'

'Oh my! Oh dear! Oh God!'

Squiffy couldn't contain himself any longer. His mirth over spilt like a rampant tidal wave, as he doubled over in fits of laughter, tears running down his face.

'Ha! Ha! Ha!'

'Oh dear oh dear!'

Hysteria had quite plainly gripped him...

In a somewhat rash turn of speed the Reverend grabbed a nearby coal shovel and descended on the burning breeches with a thunderous burst of energy…

T-H-W-A-P-P!

Dark embers of cloth rose from the fireplace.

T-H-W-A-P-P! T-H-W-A-P-P! T-H-W-A-P P!

Percival Peabody vented his frustrations on the offending trousers with great gusto.

He paused to survey the diminishing inferno, which was, in fact, quite out and had been out since the first clout of the coal shovel.

Nevertheless Percy felt much better and Squiffy at that point thought it wiser to perhaps not laugh too much more just in case.

Percy picked up his trousers and peered at the singed hole in the seating area of his breeches…

He could see daylight.

On a scale of 1 to 10, probably an 8, in hole sizes the damage was resembling the aftermath of a well targeted cannon barrage from an ancient 'ship of the line'.

Indeed, he was fairly sure that you could shoot a football through the gap without touching the charred sides.

'Never mind, old chap,' muttered Squiffy, having regained control of his various functions 'you'll go down in history as the first bowler to do a moonie!'

With that he burst out into hysterical laughter and had to reach for the brandy very quickly… for medicinal purposes!

Reverend Percival Peabody sighed deeply and sat down with his now empty teacup extended in his hand.

If you can't beat them, join them, he thought and today really was a very difficult day…

Then he remembered the lawnmower.

Oh dear!

* * * *

A few hours later a much drier Percival Peabody emerged from the front door of the Presidential Palace, home to The Rt Hon. Ronald 'Squiffy' Regis.

Percy felt decidedly warmer on the inside after several of Squiffy's 'special' teas, he had borrowed some spare clothes, the rain had stopped and there was absolutely no sign of the vicarage cat whatsoever.

A flash of colour caught Percy's eye and he glanced upward towards the front gate as the rather jolly figure of Molly Coddle, spinster of the parish, stepped cautiously around the diminishing puddles.

'Good morning Molly,' said Percy, trying not to startle the somewhat nervous club tea lady, as he noted her large basket from which emerged the jingle jangle of the much cherished club teacups and saucers.

Molly was known to while away her winter nights polishing, cleaning, dusting, and even hoovering the crockery and tea service until it sparkled liked fresh water in the bright sunshine.

Apparently she thought that her meandering towards dull and uneventful tasks would perhaps discourage the advances of one or two of the more amorous club members whose virility had not diminished with their advancing years.

Molly sighed, mindful of last year when she had been pursued around the club green by a celebratory captain on the Reverend's pushbike following the end of season celebrations.

'Good afternoon Revd Peabody,' she replied at length, with a somewhat disapproving look at the Reverend's state of dress and demeanour.

Percy glanced at his watch...

Dear God, was that really the time?

The hands stared back ominously....

Ten minutes past two o'clock!

'Er so it is.....' stuttered Percy.

'Funny how you lose track of time when visiting the parishioners.'

'Indeed,' exclaimed Molly, 'some more than others!'

Percy fell into step alongside the tea lady and together they stepped through the open club gate and into full view of the clubhouse and green.

The club was a hive of activity: numerous members were tidying the gardens, weeding the margins, cleaning windows and hanging up the outside signs in preparation.

Indeed, fully half the club were active in one way or another and the Reverend beamed with delight at such an energetic display of community spirit.

Perhaps this was going to be a good season after all.

Miss Coddle exchanged mild pleasantries at the clubhouse entrance, skilfully evading a playful tap on the bottom from Bernard, club chairman and a bit of a ladies' man by all accounts.

Percy couldn't help but notice the rather brightly coloured hat Molly sported on her brow, a splendid, almost riotous blend of red, yellow, green and blue stripes finished in a hand-knitted wool pattern.

It was almost bold enough to be a teapot cosy he mused and Percy sneaked a second glance in the direction of Molly's head.

His earlier suspicions were quickly confirmed: Miss Coddle had turned up in her Sunday best and the club tea cosy.

Reverend Peabody smiled inwardly, not having the heart to bring this delicate matter to her attention, but was left to ponder on the whereabouts of her real hat.

'Afternoon Reverend!'

The call came from a number of sources in the garden and clubhouse as various members noted his presence and paid their gracious respects.

'Good afternoon, good afternoon, what an absolute delight to see you all,' exclaimed Percy.

Percy took a few minutes to warmly greet his parishioners.

Douglas Doolittle, vice chairman, looked up from the bed of freshly planted primulas with a mixture of feigned surprise and delight which soon turned into unexpected pain as his plump posterior encountered the thorny defence of the nearby rose bed.

Bernard, always keen to use any opportunity to grab a tea break, took immediate advantage of the temporarily disabled vice chairman and the arrival of the Reverend.

'Fancy a cuppa, Percy?' he said quickly, and, steering Percy by the elbow, propelled him firmly and effectively in pursuit of Molly Coddle's tea cosy.

In the kitchen, Molly Coddle, spinster of the parish, was already hard at work.

Blissfully unaware of the impending danger approaching from behind, she was bending head first under the counter and ferreting around the dark interiors of the clubhouse cupboards.

Dust already rose into the air freely, amid the rising steam of the large water boiler, as Molly's determined foray in the kitchen storage rapidly turned into a solo vendetta against grime, grease and the world's largest spider.

Bernard chuckled.

Molly's ankle-length plastic apron had risen up an indiscreet two inches and her inch-thick 40 denier woolly tights were unwisely exposed in all their wrinkled glory.

Never one to miss the opportunity for a 'bit of a lark', Bernard tipped a wink at Jack Tuttle who already reposed in the rather large and luxurious armchair in the bar area.

Jack, or 'Big Jim' as he was known to his friends, was a retired county president, now enjoying the less demanding and more entertaining role of being the club's honorary competition secretary.

He had, over his years as president, gained a remarkable reputation for a dry and eloquent sense of humour; indeed his 'short stories' were almost a legend from board room to dinner speeches.

His appetite for comedy was, in fact, only slightly less than his appetite for good food and good wine which is why his rapidly growing waistline required the benefit of a robust armchair.

His cheery expression was surmounted by a rather red nose that would have easily gained him a place as a 'stand in' for Rudolph should Santa Claus have ever experienced transport problems again.

'Here you are, Percy,' said Bernard as he innocently directed Percy toward a neighbouring chair.

'Have a chat with Jack about this season's fixtures and I'll get the tea... how would you like it?'

Percy paused briefly as he settled into the chair and prompted a 'white with two sugars.'

Jack, awakened from his slumber at the mention of a possible drink, immediately quipped in...

'And I'll have a double!'

Percy chuckled.

With the Reverend safely installed in the company of the competition secretary, and with the rest of the club, he noted, still tidying up outside, Bernard stepped back towards the kitchen counter, now lost in Molly's adaptation of a Saharan dust storm.

Molly Coddle had no idea at all what was on the immediate horizon; in fact, with all the dust removed, she still pursued the spider with great gusto around the cupboard recesses.

'Got you!' she exclaimed with a firm, determined and successful shout, as her brush and dustpan finally, safely secured the runaway mammoth.

It was hard to piece together the actual order of events that preceded the impending disaster...

In fact, no one in their right mind could have possibly conceived the enactment of a Greek wedding ritual in the quiet confines of their clubhouse.

Several things happened all at once, almost like a chain of events leading to an inevitable conclusion, but faster than spontaneous combustion.

Bernard was, understandably, not fully cognitive to the impending disaster he was about to unleash and therefore without further consideration he gave Molly's rump a playful slap and asked in a cheerful but rather loud voice...

'How about a cuppa for the Reverend and a kiss for the plumber?'

Molly Coddle arose with an alacrity that would have put the launch of the space shuttle to shame, but unfortunately the underneath of the counter had other ideas...

B-A-N-G!

Molly's head collided with the top shelf, rattling the crockery, detaching her tea cosy and consigning one or two saucers to the floor with a resounding clatter!

The Reverend looked around with alarm!

Jack simply turned, raised his empty glass and cheerily shouted,

'Game on, Bernard!'

Now all would have gone fairly well at that point had the descending Miss Coddle not landed squarely on the dustpan and brush.

The larger than life arachnid ascended much like an Olympic gymnast, somersaulting three times before plummeting vertically towards a safe haven...

Unfortunately the safe haven proved to be Molly Coddle's tightly buttoned cardigan, now remiss of two top buttons.

The spider descended, legs akimbo, down Miss Coddle's cleavage!

To say that Molly went berserk is an understatement; some might have compared her performance with that of a Tasmanian devil.

Certainly the aftermath gave witness to the possibility of a class four tornado having rampaged through the kitchen area.

Molly Coddle stood up very, very quickly!

She stood up beating her chest like a miniature King Kong, desperate to squash the spider that was gaining intimate knowledge of her much treasured World War II corset!

The kitchen shelf, which had been resting above her, parted company with its support post at the end nearest to Molly's eruption and the neatly stacked plates, saucers, cups and teapots slid majestically along the now acute angle before plunging earthward much like the Titanic on its final descent.

C-R-A-S-H-H-H!

Bernard looked on in horror, aghast, as his friendly slap on the rump unfurled into a disaster before his eyes, disproportionate to his innocent tomfoolery.

Jack, reclining in the comfort of the luxurious armchair, was, prior to the arrival of the spider, fairly well settled and had already begun to drift off into a peaceful snooze in the warmth of the sunshine blazing through the clubhouse windows...

His slumber was abruptly, rudely interrupted by the arrival of 60 items of crockery on the flagstone floor.

Jack, known to his friends as 'Big Jim' for obvious reasons, wasn't the type of person to awaken gently.

Indeed there is no easy way to awaken 22 stone of slumbering bowler.

And Jack definitely awoke!

He transcended the void from fast asleep to wide awake in 0.5 seconds exactly!

He awoke with a crash and a clatter, rocking the table violently as the nearby kitchen tea service expanded from a 60 piece to a 600-piece service in a matter of seconds.

The table, not used to such volatile disturbances, creaked alarmingly as it wobbled precariously on its one centre leg. The small bottle of brandy nestling safely in the centre was not so forgiving.

It wobbled…

It teetered…

It started to fall over and its sweet golden contents began to trickle, and then pour onto the table with a glugging sort of sound that would horrify even the remotest and mildest of drinkers.

Jack was not an alcoholic, far from it, but he did enjoy his favourite tipple and at £90 a bottle he was not about to stand by, or even sit by, and watch it go to waste.

With an alacrity not known to many, especially to Jack, his large hand made a swoop for the falling bottle.

Had he closed his hand as it made contact with the bottle he may after all have saved the day but Jack was still sluggish from his afternoon nap and a wee dram or two had of course helped him on his way.

He made contact with his favourite tipple much like a batsman might connect with an approaching ball when he had it in mind to 'go for a six'.

The bottle left the table in a hurry.

Actually, it went into orbit, accelerating away from Jack's hand and with a sharp tinkling crash emerged victorious on the other side of the clubhouse window, or the former window as was now the case.

The Reverend looked on in complete astonishment.

The entire club membership outside in the garden looked on in even greater astonishment.

Douglas Doolittle, vice chairman, watched in dismay as the now descending projectile rapidly approached the fragile regions of his unprotected head, and did the only thing any one could do.

He ducked very quickly... and for the second time in one day his plump posterior encountered the rather thorny problem of his prize rose bush.

Douglas screamed out in pain.

The bottle swiftly re-entered the atmosphere, plunged earthward and impacted the ground with a cavernous thud!

It was still miraculously intact and with half its contents amazingly retained.

The remnants of the aforementioned window fell to the ground, sounding almost deafening in the absolute silence that had befallen the club members.

Jack sat down heavily, breathing a sigh of relief and stated the obvious.

'By Jove, that's a stroke of luck!'

Bernard sniggered.

He couldn't help it, but he didn't snigger for long!

Molly Coddle, emerging from the debris of her beloved kitchen, had finally got to grips with the rampaging arachnid and, with a lengthy frightened scream, hooked the spider out of her corset and into space.

It landed fair and square dead centre of a white bowling cap.

The bowling cap unfortunately was fair and square on the centre of Bernard's head.

Grabbing the first thing she could lay her shaking hands on Molly swept into action with a very imposing silver tea tray.

T-W-A-N-GGG!

'Got you!' she shouted at the top of her voice, turning the tray and cap into a neat sandwich with the spider very much the filling.

T-W-A-N-G! T-W-A-N-G! T-W-A-N-G!

Molly wanted to be absolutely sure that the frightful creature was no longer of this world and just maybe the fact that Bernard was wearing the cap inspired her repeat performance.

Bernard groaned loudly.

The Reverend Percival Peabody sat down heavily, his hands rising to his head, groaned loudly, deeply, into his palms and muttered a '*Hail Mary*' or two.

This was, after all, not even the very first day of the season.

CHAPTER TWO
MAY

THE SEASON'S
FIRST DAY

Percy looked around and sighed.

He often sighed but this today was a sigh of relief and expectation.

The grass was safely mown, the verges trim, the garden was resplendent in its floweriest finery, bees buzzed, birds swooped and even the tap, tap, tap of the window repairers fitting the new beading did little to spoil the moment.

The start of the season had arrived and with it the promise of good weather had been realised and the opportunity of a first day 'roll up' rested firmly on its laurels.

The first day was always taken as a friendly 'free for all' as a fair number of the members had not bowled through the winter period and those that had would be in for the usual shock as they switched from the fast carpet to the slow grass.

Then of course there were the newcomers…

All in all, the first day was a great way to welcome in the new season with warmth and friendliness and a feeling of goodwill, camaraderie and team spirit.

Remembering the previous year, Percy had no doubt that there would be more than a fair share of team spirit consumed in the bar before, during and after the roll up as well.

The problem was, as always, that old rivalries were never left behind in the preceding season, but nursed affectionately like a festering wound during the cold winter months, only to erupt into the new one with the usual results.

Old scores were yet to be settled and time had transformed previous winning results into wildly exaggerated triumphs.

Narrow victories by one or two points suddenly became huge defeats, massacres or even whitewashes in the memory of the victor who was always keen to remind the vanquished as soon as they arrived at the clubhouse.

Every year sorrows were drowned, battle lines were drawn in the threadbare grass, and campaigns were undertaken with more strategy than Rommel and more cunning than a clever magician (even one as talented as Paul Daniels!)

Most certainly, there was some out and out flouting, even violations, of every rule under the sun.

Of course there were 'by the book' players who had memorised every rule, every regulation and every required measurement, code of dress and order of play dating back to Sir Francis Drake's time.

There was a good chance that even Sir Francis would have been disqualified when competing against these players!

Then of course there was the 'old school', the bowlers whose lineage at the club predated the longest reigning succession of monarchs in history. Their fathers and grandfathers and great grandfathers had probably played before them at the club.

They knew every blade of grass on the green; in fact they could probably tell you how many blades of grass there were in total on the green!

Come to that, thought Percy, they had probably even given them all a name or a secret code that only they knew!

They could predict how the wind would affect a bowl as it passed the sudden shelter of a large buddleia, or deviated around a divot or even turned on a pile of worm casts.

These were a breed of bowler not to be taken lightly and any snigger in their direction by an unfledged younger person would soon be met by the usual 'fancy a roll up?' in a coarse, innocent, but rather sneaky façade.

They would usually follow up the invite with the well rehearsed and practised lines of…

'Of course I haven't bowled for a few years, trouble with the old back you see…'

'It's the old war wound that still troubles me…'

'Course a young man like you'll probably run rings around me…'

'I hope you'll give me a few shots head start.'

The confident beginner's usual mistake was of course to accept the challenge in the first place and to concede four shots, and a side bet of a fiver, before the first wood was even bowled.

The 'old timer', bent and crooked, leaning on his Zimmer frame, would suddenly straighten up, pick up his heavyweight woods and step on to the green with an eagerness that might just give the young player a premonition of what was to pass.

Needless to say, the younger only got to hold the cot twice, once at the beginning when he passed it to the 'old-un' (well let's face it, he's always going to win the toss) and then secondly when he picked it up at the end of the match, usually about 20 minutes later.

There's nothing more crestfallen than a cocky newcomer brought crashing to earth in 22 minutes, dropping five counts of four shots and eventually losing 21-1.

The old timer always shakes his hand and says…

'Hard luck, youngster, I had a bit of luck.'

Well, believe me, luck had nothing to do with it at all, and the usual rule of thumb is to always avoid anyone who looks like your granddad!

Percy sighed again in a whimsical fashion.

Then of course there were the 'new bloods' - the teenagers with a taste of county play…

Rose gardens and flowerbeds never really lasted long into the season once *they* stepped on the green.

The teenagers were always so eager to skip the block and took any opportunity when 'behind on the end' to deliver a broadside of a bowl that left scorch marks on the green and scattered every wood it hit over a 20 metre radius.

Which of course then brings us back to the flowers…

Well, they never did succeed in hitting many of the 'heads' and it was just a natural progression to the next target in line.

Bowls would pretty much steam through the formerly stunning display of chrysanthemums, tulips and cornflowers much like a giant rotivating scythe run amok on a corn field.

It was hardly any wonder that the poor green keeper Patrick Albright was nearly bald!

Percy sighed again… whimsically.

'Oh well,' he thought, 'let's make a start,' and with that the first car arrived.

Most of the members were soon there.

The selection committee, headed by the much favoured local councillor, the Rt Hon. Clifford James Johnson, all-round 'nice guy', led the way purposefully to the board room.

Vice captain Derek Dunstable, quick tempered at the best of times, was already muttering and puttering whilst waving a copy of the latest team selection lists.

Jack Tuttle, aka Big Jim, now much recovered after the experiences of the previous day, followed up the rear with his prized competition forms under one arm and his inner pocket bulging from his hip flask (kept purely for medicinal purposes, of course!)

'Good morning Reverend,' came the opening and warm introduction to the day from the councillor.

'Good morning Clifford.'

'Lovely day for it,' commented Jack.

'Not bad at all,' said Percy.

Derek muttered a grunt of acknowledgement.

'Any news of the new team selections?' piped Percy, eager as always to notch up his first game with the club, after several years in the reserves list.

GRUNT! ... from Derek.

Percy fell into step alongside the fast moving procession of committee members and tried to catch the eyes of the captain and vice captain.

It was never easy to catch Clifford's eye - after all, he was a councillor.

Catching the vice captain's eye was even harder, as one of them was made of glass!

Percy coughed politely into his hand.

Clifford slowed down and made to turn towards the Reverend, after all, assistant green keeper or not, it didn't do to be discourteous to a 'man of the cloth'.

Derek was not quite so quick to respond. His one good eye was casting an uncomfortable glare at Percy whilst his glass eye remained firmly fixed on the middle of Clifford's back.

He walked straight into the Captain...

CRASH!

'Oo-m-ph,' groaned Derek, momentarily winded.

Following up the rear quite speedily, Big Jim's rather imposing bulk took slightly longer to slow down.

It certainly didn't slow down quickly enough, mainly due to the fact that Jack's mind was already indulging in the delights of the inside flask.

CR-U-N-C-H!

The combination of Clifford stopping without warning and the arrival of Big Jim 'en masse' could only end in one result...

Derek was squashed; in fact he was very much the meat in the sandwich between two very larges slices of bread!

He gave a gurgling gasp as the air was expelled over-rapidly from his lungs and his glass eye popped out of its place of residence and landed on the green in front of Percy's feet.

Jack, feeling the crunch of glass from his breast pocket, reached up, placing his hand over his heart…

'Oh my God!'

Clifford, in the process of helping the winded vice captain, looked across in consternation and noticed the red stain spreading across Jack's previously pristine white shirt.

'Are you hurt, Jack?'

Jack looked down in surprise at the dark red stain and with typical aplomb stated the blindingly obvious…

'My goodness, I hope that's blood!'

He smirked and fished the broken hip flask out…

'Ha Ha Ha!' chortled Clifford, as always seeing the immediate and obvious hilarity to any situation.

Derek of course was not so happy; he was still squashed and trying to catch his second breath.

He realised that part of his anatomy was no longer attached to his body, or more to the point he was wide legged and eyeless.

Percy, trying to restore some decorum to the vice captain's predicament, perhaps in the hope of influencing the team selections, reached for the offending glass bauble now nestling on the second rink.

One would be advised at that point to well remember the club motto…whatever can go wrong probably will.

The nearby rhododendron shrubbery shook in a subtle way, a few drops of dew falling to the ground as one or two leaves were discreetly, cautiously moved.

A large, rather bushy object unfurled into a tense, quivering, expectant column rising between the leaves.

If anyone had looked closely at the mysterious shape for more than a few seconds it might have occurred to them that it somewhat resembled the tail of a very bushy cat, but then the enclosed clubhouse didn't own a cat!

Rollo, after his previous escapades, had risen early from the vicarage that morning and, noting his owner's departure, had simply done what all cats tend to do... he followed him!

Slipping through the five-bar clubhouse gate he had proceeded to enjoy the next hour touring the delights of the well manicured gardens, chasing numerous bees, butterflies and assorted shadows before settling under the nearest bush for a cat nap.

He was still at that point feeling very energetic, his whiskers sensitised, his ears perked and tail twitched as with one eye partially open he slumbered...

Something round and sparkling fell to the ground, the light reflecting off it in such a way as to catch the corner of his eye.

It bounced once or twice, arousing his curiosity, and then rolled to a stop against a worm cast.

Rollo watched...

Rollo waited...

Rollo began to get impatient...

His tailed twitched then twitched again, violently…

There's nothing worse than arousing the anticipation of a cat with a moving object and then it not moving any more.

The object continued to refuse to budge.

Percy coughed discreetly and turned towards Derek.

'I think you might have lost your marbles, my friend,' he commented, biting his tongue as his brusque dry humour kicked in.

Derek glared, opened his mouth to snap some rude comment, then wisely thought better of it and stomped past the Reverend towards the place where Percy pointed.

Rollo's tail rose high into the air as his back legs lifted, his back arched and his rear end began to shake and shimmy like a vibrating conveyer belt.

Derek stepped onto the green, not pausing to consider the fact that he still wore his working shoes, which were certainly not standard footwear for a pristinely kept bowling green.

He might have got away with the patterned sole, but the heel was another matter entirely.

Over by the clubhouse Patrick 'Postie' Albright, the green keeper, who always kept one eye on his prize grass, started to turn a pale shade of jade from the neck up; in fact he began to look very pasty as Derek strove forward ominously and stepped off the bank.

Patrick picked up the nearby broom and took a big stride forward towards him…

'Oooooooooooy!' he shouted…

'Get your big clodhoppers off my green,' he yelled as the vice-captain's left foot alighted on the hallowed turf.

Derek turned in stride, suddenly aware of his predicament as his remaining good eye affixed on the sight of the now crimson, wrathful green keeper heading swiftly towards him with broom handle raised above his head.

Rollo was rapidly reaching the point of no return and was oblivious to anything else in the immediate vicinity, including the rather large bumblebee nesting in his left ear.

His eyes glazed over with a look of typical cat insanity as he not so much reached the point but accelerated past it at a rate of knots.

He took off like a V2 rocket, propelling himself forward through the shrubbery much like a snowball's reaction to landing on a hotplate.

The rhododendron shook violently, petals flying into the air, and a very large, very hairy, very excited maniacal cat emerged at top speed.

Rollo's sole intent was to reach the enticing inanimate object in the shortest possible time.

The bee hung on for dear life!

The most direct route took him straight under the descending foot of the now troubled vice captain.

With his attention distracted by the impending threat of the approaching green keeper, off balance and looking the wrong way, the sudden arrival of a huge fur ball in full flight took Derek off guard.

Alarmed, he paused in mid-step momentarily, but, with his body weight fully committed, his pendulum-like rhythm carried his momentum forward and he began to reach the point of instability.

Totally oblivious to all the impending carnage Rollo arrived at the glass eye and proceeded, with great delight, to tap it at full tilt from one paw to another in rapid succession, much as if he was playing an arcade game.

He charged across the green like John McEnroe on drugs, patting the bauble back and forth at high speed, almost falling over himself in the excitement of the chase.

An ear splitting shout caught his attention as, for the first time, he registered the impression of a furious red apparition charging towards the green.

Patrick 'Postie' Albright was in full charge and he was a man on a mission.

The broom handle waved dangerously above his head.

Phillippa Spindleforth, until then enjoying an early morning cup of Earl Grey, sat on the bench nearby looking rather perplexed.

She could not, for the life of her, work out why a coarse bristled broom head was now nestling, detached, on her new perm.

On a scale of 1 to 10 Rollo registered a 9 on the panic scale and all thought of participating in a game of pat-a-cake with the glass eye suddenly evaporated.

Rollo put on the brakes...

His front paws splayed out two sets of very imposing razor-sharp claws and dug in...

His rear end was slightly slower in reacting and tumbled riotously over his head, propelling him backwards at high speed, his front claws etching two sets of evenly matched tramlines into the grass.

Looking upside down between his splayed open rear legs the vision of a now inverted green keeper, enraged, waving a broom handle and approaching with gusto was simply too much for an over-taxed vicarage cat.

Rollo did what all cats usually do when threatened, but then Rollo was no ordinary cat…

His hackles rose like those of a rampant porcupine, quadrupling his size in two seconds flat, his tail did a very good impression of a giant loo brush and he let out a very anguished

'M-e-o-o-o-wwww!'

The bee, thoroughly disgruntled, disorientated and disturbed had had enough!

He buzzed angrily in Rollo's left ear, stung him once, and buzzed off!

'Meeeeeeooooowwww!'

Rollo left the ground in a vertical direction, rising like a Harrier jump jet, rotated 180 degrees and hit the ground running.

To be fair, his flight would have given him every opportunity to record a record-breaking three-minute mile, such was his speed of departure and Rollo, throbbing ear and all, was in FULL flight.

His razor-like claws dug at the ground, pushing him forward faster and faster, a cloud of newly pruned grass shoots rising like a cloud behind him.

A previously unnoticed mound appeared before him and, as all cats do, he continued on unabated, straight up the side of the cloth covered shape, his claws embedding deeply into the soft yielding material.

Derek screamed very, very loudly...

'A-a-a-r-r-g-h!'

The needle-like claws left a trail of acupuncture marks up Derek's leg and back in quick succession as Rollo arrived at the mount summit in record time.

'Ouch! Ouch! Ouch! Ouch! Ouch!' stuttered Derek in quick-fire staccato.

A much maligned vicarage cat now perched precariously on the top of the vice chairman's head, his legs stiff, back arched, fur raised in alarm, spitting, hissing and caterwauling in an ear-splitting fashion.

Derek teetered.

Percy looked on in amazement, slack jawed, eyes wide and speechless.

Big Jim, overcome with merriment, chortled outrageously and fell to the ground helpless as a newborn baby, overcome with hysterics.

Patrick pulled to a halt; the broom handle paused in mid-threat.

Phillippa looked up from beneath the bristles and piped up,

'Anyone for tea?'

Derek groaned and sat down very heavily.

The vicarage cat had begun to calm down.

His ear still throbbed painfully of course!

Rollo sat down in a shapeless mass vaguely resembling a Davy Crockett hat and began to purr cautiously in a nervous fashion, his claws pulsing as they kneaded the top of Derek's scalp.

* * * *

Some time later normal service had been resumed, with the arrival of a very large pot of tea, a few sticky plasters, a wee dram for Big Jim (and a clean shirt of course!), a couple of tranquillisers and a large bowl of premium cat food.

The selection committee had by now retired *en masse* to the office, which was, quite appropriately, midway between the bar and the kitchen.

Here they would discuss, barter, wage war, take sides, stipulate rules, issue demands, bribe, corrupt and otherwise use every trick in the book to obtain the best players for their favourite teams.

Back at the clubhouse several of the members were settling down over a nice cuppa, cautiously eyeing up the newcomers and keeping tabs on the level of chocolate biscuits in the Tupperware container.

One or two of the more experienced individuals had a severe case of 'itchy finger' and were dying to get out onto the newly opened and pristine bowling green.

In the corner nearest the bar (well, it was always the one closest to the bar mainly due to the fact that a certain member liked to exercise every opportunity for a free pint) sat Bernard 'Batty' Bartrum and Dennis 'Sticky' Ditherford.

Bernard, nicknamed 'Batty' because he definitely was a bit, and Dennis, aka 'Sticky' because he often resembled a stick insect when he delivered his bowl, sat talking in hushed tones.

Batty and Sticky were the club's answer to Batman and Robin of the bowling green, both former champions on many occasions, and always seemingly able to use their super-powers to win through on the day.

True, these super-powers included the more dubious skills of talking too much, being over-critical, pleading any and all injury and use of a highly debatable method of 'measuring for shot' when the outcome of the game was in question.

Indeed, their performances would really have earned them a standing ovation had they been acted out on a West End stage and perhaps they had more in common with the Joker and the Riddler given their oratory skills.

Bernard and Dennis had been very good friends for a very long while and were of course partners in any and every team game conceivable.

At this point in time they were eager to get on the green and begin the season with a good win, therefore they were, typically, weighing up the usual suspects and the unknown quantities to see who would make the most likely candidate for a good thrashing.

Sitting apart from the crowd were two fairly young, and obviously new, participants to the game. They were looking around slightly uncomfortably, probably due to the fact that they were 40 years younger than anyone else in the clubhouse at that particular moment.

Paul Jenner was a typical quiet teenager, the son of the not so quiet Pauline Jenner who was a 'wannabe' mother in as much as she wanted to be in favour with everyone and was never backward in coming forward, to the point of extreme bluntness.

In fact her manner was often abrasive enough to have removed the top coat off a door frame quicker than a triple-strength paint stripper.

Anyway, getting back to the plot, which was about to thicken, Paul sat enjoying a double shot of Fanta and wondering what to do next.

His newly discovered friend was none other than Johnny Jackson, an unknown to the club and indeed the area having just moved there about a month ago.

Paul and Johnny were having a deep and meaningful conversation about the key things in life: girls, drink, dance music and pizzas, therefore the conversation tended to ebb and flow in sentences of no more than 10 words at a time.

Bernard looked across to his friend Dennis and tipped him the wink…

'Here we go, Dennis, those two young 'uns look like they'll be easy meat. Young Paul only joined the club this year and that new guy isn't much older than him.'

Dennis looked casually over his shoulder, pretending to inspect the fraying corner of his old shirt, and weighed up the youngsters.

He turned back and smiled.

'Well?' said Bernard.

'I think we'll go and invite the lads to a friendly roll up,' chuckled Dennis, with a sly look in his eye.

Dennis stood up in a frail sort of stance, Bernard did likewise, and with empty cups rattling slightly in their 'arthritically induced' hands they made their way towards the kitchen counter.

Their slightly precarious journey was noted by several of the more knowledgeable club members who smirked silently and looked away to smother their amusement in their own early morning tea.

Batty and Sticky, the long-serving former club champions with more than 60 years, playing experience between them, arrived at the new boys' table.

'Good morning lads,' said Bernard, 'I guess you'll be eager to get out on to the green for your first game?'

'Of course we don't play as much as we used to now we've retired,' piped up Dennis.

'Anyway, you youngsters could probably run rings around us old-uns,' continued Bernard, trying desperately not to snigger.

Dennis, with a face only slightly more controlled, finished the conversation…

'We'd be honoured if you'd consider giving us the privilege of your company for a couple of hours, it'll be nice to have a bit of a game so how about if we challenge you both to a friendly pairs match.'

The clubhouse door swung open and Patrick 'Postie' Albright stepped in.

'Ok ladies and gentlemen, the greens are open for play, it's opening day so club dress code please, with ties whilst committee are all here.'

He paused for breath then continued…

'Rinks one to six for ladies and men's club morning leagues, seven and eight for anyone wishing to practise '

Bernard spoke up in a wheezy voice....

'We'll take rink eight if we can, Patrick. These youngsters have just challenged us to a pairs match!'

Patrick looked suspiciously at Bernard, and opened his mouth as if to say a few words, then looked at Paul and Johnny's slightly bewildered faces and closed his mouth again with a slight smirk.

'Ok, I'll put out some mats and a cot for you on the rink,' said Patrick, struggling to hold back the look of mirth that was flickering across his weather-beaten features.

With that he shut the door again.

Bernard turned to the youngsters and with slightly more enthusiasm in his voice commented...

'Well, we'll see you boys on the green in 10 minutes then.'

And then with an afterthought Dennis said 'As it's your first day and game we'll put in your rink fees for you.'

They headed towards the door, their step all the more brisk. After all, a couple of pounds each was nothing when compared with the pleasure of leading another two lambs to the slaughter.

What's more, they had played most of the season every year on rink eight, their favourite, which also happened to be a difficult end rink with lots of unusual 'straights' and 'runs' which only they knew.

'Oh well,' said Johnny, 'I guess we'd better not disappoint them.

How do you feel?'

'I reckon we've just been led up the garden path,' muttered Paul, 'although I have had some coaching during the last couple of years.'

'Well, I hope they're not counting their chickens too soon,' smiled Johnny and stood up ready to head off to the changing rooms.

Paul followed suit and together they went off to get ready.

As they departed, Patrick stepped past them back into the clubhouse.

The green keeper headed towards the bar chuckling to himself under his breath until he reached the teapot, paused to pour a fresh brew, then, in the process of adding sugar, started to laugh lightly, unable to hold back his mirth.

'Hee hee hee' he chortled gleefully under his breath.

'Oh dear! Oh crumbs!' he snorted. 'Ha! Ha! Ha! Ha!' he smirked, tears running down his bright cheeks as he doubled over the counter in fits of laughter.

'Oh come on, Patrick,' piped up one of the many members having tea…

'We know it's funny Bernard and Dennis getting up to their usual tricks, but ought we to warn the lads?'

Patrick looked round at the many smiling faces.

'Oh dear lord…' he chuckled, 'that's not what's so funny!'

'I say, old chap, come on then, spill the beans' spouted Chalkie.

Eric 'Chalkie' Tunstall was a fairly decent bowler and had been with the club quite a number of years following his early retirement from the Royal Air Force where he'd been a commercial pilot under contract for many years.

Patrick took a deep breath, a quick slurp of his hot cup of tea, and pulled himself together,

'Well, Paul's been getting some serious coaching over the last couple of years before joining us.' he said.

'Yes, well, that's all well and good,' butted in Bertie Tattleford, always one for barging in with a few choice words...'but he's still no match for Bernard and Dennis!'

'Well that's just the point,' said Patrick, 'he's playing with Johnny Jackson!'

Patrick looked around the room at the quizzical expressions on the member's faces and realised that the proverbial penny was not dropping.

'Johnny Jackson used to play for Norfolk Bowling Club...'

The members looked around at each other, still not fully comprehending, although they knew that Norfolk Bowling Club had a fine reputation as one of the other counties' top clubs.

But still the penny refused to drop...

Patrick sighed with a combination of a smirk, a snigger and an exasperated 'matter of fact' expression on his face.

'Johnny Jackson,' he said, 'has played for the Norfolk county side for 10 years and was the youngest ever player to be nominated for the under-25's England team!'

Silence descended upon the clubhouse.

'And…' Patrick continued.

'Last year he won the British junior singles title!'

The penny dropped… in fact it not so much dropped but went down faster than a large lead weight in a swimming pool.

A titter from Eric started them off, then a raucous guffaw from the explosive Bertie and within seconds the clubhouse filled with a wave of infectious laughter.

'Ha! Ha! Ha!'

'Oh dear…'

'Hee hee hee!'

'Oh by Jove, that's rich!'

'Ha ha ha ha ha…'

The assorted comments bounced around the room with merriment and, as one, the members arose and headed for the door, eager to watch the proverbial 'slaughter' of the youngsters by Bernard and Dennis.

Dennis and Bernard were already on the green, comfortably dressed in well-worn grey trousers, white shirts and neckwear resembling club ties, although on closer inspection one might have noted that Bernard's sported Mickey Mouse in Disneyland and Dennis's was a Club 18-30 one.

The duo were busy polishing their woods and exchanging gleeful comments, in fact, in a fit of extreme generosity they had even put four shots up on the board on the youngsters' side, just to give them a head start.

As it was just a 'friendly' the cot was already positioned on a full length mark at the other end of the green.

The boys arrived, sporting smart new club outfits, trousers perfectly creased, shirts ironed, ties knotted, and spanking new bowls bags at their sides.

Dennis and Bernard were positively hopping with excitement like two kids on Christmas Eve having seen the huge pile of presents waiting at the foot of the Christmas tree.

A rather noisy crash distracted Dennis and Bernard's attention briefly as the clubhouse door swung open in a very solid fashion, rattling the new window, and allowing the assorted contents of members to spill out on to the veranda.

There were, in fact, nearly 30 of them, ladies and gentlemen all mixed together, tittering quietly in an exuberance of childish behaviour.

Dennis couldn't help but notice that all those that were supposed to be playing on the other rinks had seemingly given up their own games to come and watch the one now set to commence on rink eight.

Obviously the word was out!

The audience settled down on a mixture of benches, stools, sun loungers and armchairs, all hurriedly manoeuvred to allow best vantage points around the rink.

Fresh pots of tea miraculously appeared as if by magic, biscuit bowls were topped up and the members sat down to watch and wait for the surprise to be sprung.

Even Rollo, normally never a sensible proposition around the bowling green, had suppressed his candid maniacal streak and, enthused by the sense of anticipation, had settled down by the rink marker to watch the events unfurl.

Dennis turned around to Bernard with a huge grin on his face, but he couldn't help notice that Bernard was looking a little bit perplexed.

Bernard was staring intently at Johnny's tie which didn't seem to be the normal club tie, in fact the colours were something that he vaguely remembered but he couldn't for the life of him remember exactly where from.

He noted also, as Johnny removed his outer jacket, that he seemed to have some writing just above the club logo embroidered on his shirt, only it wasn't the club name but some other...

He leaned a little bit closer...

'That's a nice badge there, youngster,' said Bernard inquisitively.

'What's that for then, your last club?'

Johnny looked up at Bernard with a faint smile teasing at the edge of his mouth...

'Not really.'

Bernard paled significantly...

'Not a county badge is it?'

Johnny shook his head in a negative fashion.

'Of course not.'

Bernard breathed a sigh of relief.

'You had me going there for a second, youngster.'

It must be, after all, just a manufacturer's logo on the shirt.

Johnny continued…

'Not county... national!'

Bernard smiled broadly, laughed nervously and said with a strained voice, 'Of course it is, how silly of me.'

He paused for response and then continued…

'You'll be telling me next you're the English champion.'

'Well actually yes!' replied Johnny.

'Bernard laughed again in an unbelieving manner, but looked more closely at the shirt.

'2005 Under-25s English Bowls Champion,' read the embroidered response.

It ran in an arc over the logo…

The logo of the English Bowling Association…

The logo that matched the colours of the tie…

Bernard laughed in a strangled, hysterical fashion.

'Er…um… yes… so you are,' his voice rising a few octaves in the process.

Dennis wandered over as a cheer went up from the members watching.

'Game on, Bernard.' they called.

'Need a head start?'

'Cat got your tongue?'

'What's wrong then, met your match?'

The audience laughed loudly and Bernard groaned as he realised he'd finally been caught out at his own game.

Dennis looked at the badge and then took his partner to one side.

'Come on, Bernard, it's not that bad,' he whispered under his breath. 'There's still the two of us and they've only got the one good bowler, and no matter how brilliant he is he can't beat all of our woods single handed, can he?'

He thought for a few seconds and then perked up.

'You're right, you know,' he muttered to Dennis. 'Come on, let's go and give these teenagers a lesson in bowling.'

Sticky and Batty, now confidently reassured, walked across to Paul and Johnny, exchanged handshakes and good wishes, and then tossed a coin to see who would take first go.

'Heads!' shouted Johnny.

They all looked down... heads it was indeed!

Bernard walked surreptitiously across to the scoreboard and commented innocently, 'I'll just set the scoreboard up,' as he reclaimed the four shot lead they had left on for Paul and Johnny.

Dennis smiled and turned to Johnny:

'Come on, let's go on up the green. We'll leave these two to start the game.'

And with that Dennis and Johnny wandered off.

The audience watched expectantly.

Rollo yawned, and then raised one eyebrow in a quizzical fashion as Paul opened his bowls bag and extracted a rather large set of brand new woods.

Bernard smiled, more confidently now; after all, he knew Paul had never really played and those woods looked like they had never used.

'Been spending your birthday money, Paul?' he quipped.

Paul looked up at Bernard.

'No,' said Paul, then paused for effect...

'Actually they're a present from an uncle of mine.' He paused again...

'He thought I was ready for a proper set of woods now, after all that practice.'

Bernard suddenly felt a little bit queasy...

'Practice?' he said, 'I thought this was your...' then bit his tongue, suddenly realising he was giving too much information away.

'Well, this will be my first game on this green,' said Paul, 'but I've practised nearly every night for three hours a time with my uncle for the last two years now!'

Bernard started to feel very, very uneasy after this sudden revelation.

'Oh,' he said, in an almost sarcastic sort of way.

'And you'll be telling me next your uncle is the world champion, Tony Allcock.'

Paul laughed.

'Of course not,' he replied, 'don't be silly…'

Bernard sighed.

'He's Martin King, the Norfolk national!' he said with a big smile.

Bernard groaned and started to feel very dizzy.

'Game on then.' said Paul and stepped on to the mat to deliver his first bowl.

Bernard looked on in an increasingly alarmed manner, suddenly aware that his plan had backfired in a big, BIG way.

Paul delivered the bowl with a graceful fluid motion.

The bowl travelled easily along the inner edge, curving inward as it reached the far end of the green, tipped towards the jack and trailed it cleanly into the ditch.

'Well, that's a bit of luck!' exclaimed Paul as he stepped off the mat with a large smile on his face.

Bernard sat down on the grass bank with a long groan as the audience applauded the shot and realised that this was one game he was never going to forget.

It was a reticent Bernard and Dennis who crawled into the clubhouse two hours later.

They had done their best and made a fight of it, but the energy, enthusiasm, keenness and level of play had given the youngsters the edge, of that there was no doubt.

And so it was grudgingly but with respect that Sticky and Batty accepted defeat with a shake of the hand and a final glance at the scoreboard -21-11- which reflected that just for once the best had been beaten, caught at their own game, hoisted, as it were, on their own petard.

Paul and Johnny stepped into the clubhouse amid a rousing cheer and shouts of 'Well done' and 'Good show' and 'Long overdue'.

Johnny looked across to the crestfallen couple and offered an olive branch... 'Fancy a drink, you two?'

Well, the offer of a freshly pulled pint was always something to smile about and, never ones to look a gift horse in the mouth, Bernard and Dennis swiftly quick-stepped to the bar in a very positive fashion.

Bernard opened his mouth to utter a few gracious words but never had the opportunity, as the clubhouse door swung open and the selection committee rolled in.

Derek, Clifford and Jack, looking very officious, which was hard to do after two hours sitting by the spirits cabinet, walked across to the notice board with a healthy glow and a resolute manner.

Patrick followed close behind and announced, in no uncertain tones, 'Place your bets, ladies and gents, the teams for this season have been selected!'

A hurried gathering and hushed overtones of healthy argumentative discussion arose as the members surrounded the selectors.

Tap! Tap! Tap! Tap!

Big Jim firmly pinned the list of newly selected teams to the board.

The first to read passed on the details and spurious comments to those less fortunate and not yet able to see.

'Well done, Russell, you're blue team captain again.'

'Hello Chalkie, you've been promoted to skip a block.'

'Looks like you're in the blue league, Charlie!'

'Well done, Percy, you're in at last, you're playing with Bertie and 'Trigger' in the orange league!'

Percy's heart soared briefly with excitement…

'At last!' he thought to himself, at last an opportunity to bowl for the club…

THE MEN'S TEAM GETS POSTED

RED TEAM   Captain - Clifford Johnson

A SQUAD

Lead	David Dimpley
No. 2	Eric 'Chalkie' Tunstall
No. 3	Clifford James Johnson
Skip	Jack 'Big Jim' Tuttle
Reserve	James 'Scottie' McCarver

B SQUAD

Lead	Paul Jenner
No. 2	Bernard 'Batty' Bartrum
No. 3	Johnny Jackson
Skip	Dennis 'Sticky' Ditherford
Reserve	Frenchie 'Wide Boy' Phillips

BLUE TEAM   Captain - Russell Cobblethwaite

Lead	Charles 'Charlie' Chesterford
No. 2	Douglas Doolittle
No. 3	Patrick 'Postie' Albright
Skip	Russell Cobblethwaite
Reserve	Colin Spindleforth

ORANGE TEAM   Captain - Derek Dunstable

Lead	Percival 'Percy' Peabody
No. 2	Tony 'Trigger' Havershall
No. 3	Bertie Tattleford
Skip	Derek Dunstable
Reserve	Reginald Trimley

Tony was OK, a bit slow on the uptake of course, in fact he could be very dim at times, and Bertie was a real handful when over-excited, which was quite often, he mused quietly to himself.

'Who's the orange league captain?' shouted Percy above the chit-chat, gossip and background noise.

There was a brief pause and then Derek turned around with his glass eye fixed penetratingly on Percy's eager face...

'I am!' he said with a smile that spoke volumes and wouldn't have looked out of place in a dental surgery on a Sunday morning.

'Oh dear,' muttered Percy and said a quick *'Hail Mary'* under his breath.

'Who's in the red team?' someone called out...

The red team were the pinnacle of bowling in Lower South-borough to which all aspired; their key players bonded in two squads which would represent the club at a number of county, league and challenge events during the course of the season.

'Clifford, David, Jack and Eric are the first squad!' called out Dennis who had now wriggled his way to the front, which was fairly easy for a man of his slight build.

'Bernard, you're with me in the second squad!' shouted Dennis, looking for his old stable mate and partner with a happy grin on his face.

Bernard looked across, happy at least that the season would be set for the 'Old School' team reunion tour once again.

'Who's with us?' he shouted back.

Dennis turned and looked again then fell silent...

'Well?' shouted Bernard.

Dennis coughed, looked across and with a slight tightness to his throat said...

'Er... um... well... we're with Paul and Johnny...'

Bernard groaned as the rest of the room cheered and clapped and laughed at the announcement.

'Never mind, old chap,' said Johnny as he walked over and slapped Bernard in a firm friendly manner on the back. 'At least we're all on the same side.'

Bernard thought briefly, taking in the words, and then perked up rather quickly.

'By God, you're right,' he said.

'We'll make a fine team between us...'

He thought further for a few seconds and then hurried after Johnny as his mind stepped into high gear.

'I say, Johnny, how about entering the club competition fours together?'

Johnny smiled at Paul and winked.

'How about county competitions?' Bernard shouted.

The bit was now firmly between his teeth as his brain begun to work overtime.

All those possibilities!

All those opportunities!

What a team...

What a combination...

'Why, they could win the county competitions…' he mused.

They might even get an opportunity to play on the hallowed turf of Worthing...

Bernard raced after Paul and Johnny.

'I say… Johnny.'

He called again…

'Johnny!'

But Paul and Johnny were already lost in the throng, heading towards the kitchen for refreshments amid lots of celebratory comments and kind wishes.

Bernard put his arm around Dennis and guided him back to the main bar...

'Well, my old friend, we learnt a valuable lesson today and maybe, just maybe, this is going to be a golden year for our squad.' And with that final thought he ordered a couple of brandies.

Dennis nearly fell over at the shock of Bernard ordering a round, but recovered quickly enough to make the most of it...

'Make mine a double,' he said.

CHAPTER THREE
JUNE
THE COUNTY
CALL-UP

Percy sighed...

He seemed to do that a lot before any big event, which coincidently seemed to pre-empt the beginning of every month between April and September.

June was the beginning of the serious season, when preliminary rounds of county competitions were battled through and won or lost, club competitions were drawn out of the hat, and touring teams began their annual pilgrimage across neighbouring counties.

The club captain, the Rt Hon. Clifford James Johnson, with the invaluable resources of his esteemed position in the council, had arranged for the neighbouring county to participate in a charity challenge competition.

The highly publicised event was due to raise funds for several deserving causes, including a children's hospice for which there was a royal patron, and rumours abounded that there might even be a royal visit on the cards.

Lower South-Borough's key players from the two red team squads were away on a whirlwind tour of the region's clubs as part of a county president's team and were not due back until late in the day.

It was a typical hazy and balmy June day, the sun was rising full in the sky already and even the birds seem happy as they flew low over the green and the slumbering form of Rollo, the vicarage cat.

Never far from the exciting and exhilarating adventures that seemed to befall the club during his every visit, Rollo had dropped in early.

He had found no one about, and in typical cat fashion had 'dropped off' where he stood, or in this case now lay curled up on the warm brass plate on the centre of the southern bank.

Percy stretched his limbs, raising his arms into the air in exuberant fashion, and yawned in a lazy drawl as the warmth of the sun passed over his body.

He was, if it could be believed, feeling rather cheerful and perhaps ever so slightly mischievous and perhaps he would have to offer a few prayers in his thoughts later and probably more than a few 'Hail Marys'.

* * * *

Percy sat outside the green keeper's shed and admired the sweeping panorama of the club grounds.

The majestic flowerbeds were now in the early stages of their summer splendour, full of colour and heady with an inviting and perfumed fragrance.

The clean cut and understated lines of the ditch and bank surrounded the perfection of a manicured, monitored and microscopically inspected lawn.

Earlier in the morning he had checked the ditches for any residual litter blown in on the breeze, swept the worm casts from the green, rotated all the rinks, trimmed any dead flower heads and was now set to rescue Molly Coddle's tea cosy from the weather vane.

He was fairly sure that with Bernard and Dennis away on tour he would have to look a lot closer to home to find the culprit of comedy who had sought to indicate the direction of north with such a multicoloured mannequin.

The tea cosy had actually looked quite funny as it flapped and inflated in colourful fashion in the early breeze.

What didn't look quite so funny was the white china pot with 14 cups and saucers that stood in line abreast, like a regiment on parade, along the apex of the club roof.

Perhaps even that would have raised a snigger or two from Percy as he pondered the identity of the latest club comedian, but the sight of Russell Cobblethwaite's thick woollen long-johns flying at half mast from the flag pole left the vicar astounded.

Russell Cobblethwaite was the club's most senior and respected veteran bowler. He was also less than conscious of fashion trends and therefore sported ill-fitting false teeth, long-johns under his bowling clothes and a somewhat worn flat cap that went out of style shortly after Elvis was born.

Those long-johns were now doing involuntary somersaults alongside Molly Coddle's tea cosy.

Percy was fairly sure that he was unlikely to see the very honourable and gentlemanly form of Russell Cobblethwaite streaking across the green. In fact it would probably take him approximately two and a half hours to traverse the green given his current stage of senility and allowing for his Zimmer frame.

Percy was also fairly sure that the much respected bowling veteran had not taken up membership of a nudist colony, nor was inclined to 'mooning' at the tea lady.

Allowing for the fact that it was not the act of a hormonally rampaging senior member in pursuit of the much desired parish spinster, Percy concluded that it could only be one thing…

Evidently the Doolittle family were at home and the youngest, Timothy (Tiny) and Abbey (Spice), were back from their boarding schools for the summer season.

Abbey would clearly spend every available opportunity trying all the contents of the lady members' make-up bags.

Probably most of it would end up on the clubhouse mirrors, glassware, trophy cabinet as well as anything white, which would cause some embarrassment for the male bowlers who ventured onto the green with red lipstick smeared all over their white shirts.

Young Timothy was a lot of teenager in a small frame, because when he arrived, mischievousness was sure to follow much like the sudden arrival of a miniature tornado.

This definitely had all the hallmarks of Timothy's handiwork. Percy sighed and untied the halyard holding the long-johns at half mast.

THUNK!

Percy heard a distracting noise and looked around but saw nothing.

CLUNK! CLUNK! CLUNK!

The noise seemed to come from above and appeared to be coming nearer.

He looked upwards with a mixture of uncertainty, bemusement and trepidation…

His immediate eye line was suddenly filled with the vision of what appeared to be a huge flying saucer appearing from nowhere.

Percy, being Percy, and prone to over-reaction, immediately over-reacted.

The molecular structure of his brain reached racing mode in a split second…with a turmoil of conflicting thoughts.

Maybe the children were having a teddy bears' picnic with their toys and tea service on the clubhouse roof.

But then that would be ridiculous.

Possibly the tea lady Molly Coddle had taken up the less popular sport of discus throwing, but that was extremely unlikely.

Conceivably, miniature space aliens were landing in their equally minute flying saucers on the bowling green, but that would be preposterous.

Perhaps one of the aircraft passing overhead had lost a small part of its anatomy such as a toilet seat.

But that would be remote and far-fetched.

Realistically it could be...

That was as far as Percy's thought processes were able to calculate, compute and consider before direct intervention from nature's irreversible mechanism responded as a matter of reaction following action.

The split second of contemplation was more than enough time for the saucer to span the gap from roof to Percy and proceed to land directly on his head.

CRASH!

The plate broke into two halves and fell to the ground with a rattling, tinkling, shattering sound as a stupefied Percy stood still.

Unfortunately the accompanying cup was not far behind.

CRASH!

And it followed suit, bouncing onto the Reverend's bald spot before ricocheting off intact like a 'Barnes Wallis' bomb and joining the aforementioned saucer in a myriad of tiny pieces as it reached ground level.

A childish titter of laughter reached his ears, and a much less magnanimous Percy looked around to discover the source of his annoyance.

Behind the clubhouse Timothy stood with a very long bamboo cane in hand, trying desperately to suppress the hysterical laughter that threatened to engulf him.

He peered around the corner to where Percy stood, or had stood, because there now remained just an empty space previously occupied by the cup, saucer and Reverend.

'Gotcha!'

The vicar's firm hand gripped the collar of Timothy's jacket, having sneaked around the far side of the clubhouse whilst 'Tiny' wasn't paying attention.

It was not the right thing for members of the clergy to get annoyed or indicate any anger, but Percy was particularly vexed and he had a very sore head.

He frogmarched the prankster around the corner, not quite sure yet what to do with the mischievous imp.

Something flapping in the breeze caught Percy's eye and a wicked smile broke across his countenance, as the much-versed cliché 'Sauce for the goose...' sprang to mind.

'Who-o-o-o-o-o-o-o-aaaah!'

Timothy called out in surprise as the Reverend propelled him upwards into the air by his collar and belt.

'Oh n-o-o-o-o-o-o…!'

Timothy descended, feet first, into Russell Cobblethwaite's long-johns, now dangling by the halyard near the grass verge.

With a rueful smile Percy pulled on the rope and 'Tiny' rose into the air, securely trapped in the woollen restraints until he hung at half-mast like a pirate in a crow's nest.

'That,' said Percy, 'Takes care of that!'

He rubbed his hands together in satisfaction and turned around…

He decided to leave Timothy there for half an hour to reflect on his childish pranks.

'Hello?'

Percy nearly jumped clear out of his skin as a rather gruff, loud and inquiring voice announced its presence.

'Hello there, I wonder if you can help us?'

The voice was very firm, obviously used to dealing with instructions and enquiries and expecting fairly decisive responses.

Percy turned round.

A rather smartly dressed, plumpish, or to be more exact 'well rounded', gentleman stood at the edge of the green.

He was resplendent in crisp white trousers, white shirt and blue jacket, garnished with a variety of badges of office and other adornments.

A large, highly impressive and much polished 'badge of office' hung in golden splendour around his neck and Percy wondered for a minute if Mr T. had mislaid any of his costume jewellery.

Standing by his side stood a rather prim and proper, posh looking woman dressed similarly but with a white panama hat adorning a striking white and purple tinged perm.

She was standing, mouth open, in a speechless state staring upwards at the 13-year-old Timothy swinging in long-johns halfway up the flagpole.

She had yet to take in the precariously balanced teacups on the roof top or the multicoloured tea cosy indicating a northerly direction or indeed why the Reverend was holding on to a 15-foot length of bamboo cane.

'The name's Tinkleton, Sir John 'Jeremiah' Tinkleton,' spouted the gentleman by way of an introduction…

'And this is my good lady wife Matilda Elizabeth Tinkleton.'

Percy looked on confusedly, but with good manners being the order of the day extended his hand in a warm greeting.

'Er… um… hello, I'm Reverend Percival Peabody, assistant green keeper…my friends call me Percy!'

'Pleased to meet you, old chap,' said Sir John.

Percy, still none the wiser, and with his hand still firmly being shaken by the gentleman visitor, looked on with an air of vagueness.

'Is there anything I can help you with?' he inquired at length.

'Snodsham,' exclaimed Sir John.

'Pardon?' said Percy.

'Snodsham!' exclaimed Sir John again, with a slightly more firm tone to his voice.

Percy by that point was beginning to feel like a freewheeling break dancer with rubber limbs as the gentleman's vice-like grip still firmly retained his own hand, pumping vigorously.

'I'm sorry, I don't understand.'

'North Snodsham ladies' touring team!' said Sir John.

'I'm the county president and their honoured guest,' he added as an afterthought.

Percy, still uncomprehending, finally extracted his squashed fingers from the grip of the now identified visitor.

He racked his mind feverishly… touring team?

'Er… you said touring team?'

Matilda Elizabeth Tinkleton decided it was time for a lady to step in and take the reins, in a manner of speaking.

'We have accepted a challenge to play against your ladies' team as part of our summer tour,' she said, in rich dulcet tones.

Realisation dawned on Percy… the North Snodsham ladies' touring team…

Of course!

They were one of the elite ladies' teams that toured every year raising money for good causes and this year they had accepted an invitation to play against Lower South-Borough's finest!

'Well, yes but… yes... of course… that's right…' stuttered Percy…

'But you are playing our ladies' team on June 11th, aren't you?'

'Yes of course,' spouted Sir John, 'quite so… I made all the arrangements myself.'

Sir John fished out a very impressive leather bound diary which had his name embossed in gold lettering across the bottom of it.

He flicked open the relevant page, marked out by a gold embroidered cloth strip.

'Here we are, Friday June 11th,' Lower South-Borough, arrive in morning, lunch, and then play at 1.00 p.m.' stated Sir John, in a very pronounced and clipped voice.

Percy looked across at Matilda Elizabeth Tinkleton in a somewhat embarrassed manner and coughed.

'Well… Um…'

Percy tried to be as tactful as he could.

'Yes, of course, we are looking forward with great pleasure to playing your team on Saturday June 11th…'

'But but but…' spluttered Sir John, 'but the match is today…Friday…'

'Friday June 11th,' he repeated…

'Look, man, look, here it is, it's written down in my diary!' he exclaimed, somewhat flustered.

Percy glanced down at the larger diary now thrust under his nose and squinted his eyes to read the bold script written in fountain pen.

Lower South-Borough, Tour Match, 1.00 p.m.

Percy frowned and looked again.

Friday June 11th.

Perplexed now, Percy took hold of the diary, now virtually hidden under his nose, removed it from Sir John's hand and reached for his reading glasses.

He checked again, more resolutely.

Lower South-Borough, Tour Match, 1.00 p.m. it read, clear as could be under the date Friday June 11th 2004.

Percy glanced over at Sir John, now resembling a preening rooster, and with a sigh pointed out the blindingly obvious to the county president.

'You've written the right details down, but in the wrong diary. This is last year's diary!'

He continued, 'June 11th may have been a Friday last year, but this year it's a Saturday!'

Sir John blinked furiously and stared down at the open pages that Percy had placed firmly in front of him.

'But! But! But!' spluttered Sir John, 'That can't be right?'

He looked, he stared, he read and re-read and he realised...

'Oh dear,' he said finally, after a few swallows.

His wife looked at him, somewhat aghast, then back again at Percy...

'But we have 24 ladies on the coach for a tour match all ready to play and we've driven 124 miles to get here…' she said at length

Percy considered quickly then made a suggestion.

'Look, why don't you bring the ladies into the clubhouse. There's plenty of hot water, tea making facilities and biscuits. There's a toilet as well. Make yourselves at home and I'll go and ring the ladies' captain to see what we can do…'

'Good idea,' said Matilda, and then a much harsher 'Come on John,' firmly grabbing his elbow… 'Let's go and tell the ladies and then you and I are going to have a 'little' talk!'

And with that she steered the rather worried looking and beetroot coloured Sir John 'Jeremiah' Tinkleton towards the coach.

'One more thing,' she inquired, looking back over her shoulder…

'Why is that young boy hanging off your flagpole in a pair of long-johns?'

Percy groaned.

* * * *

Paul, David, Eric, Clifford, Jack, James, Bernard, Johnny, Dennis and Frenchie, the cream of the crop of Lower South-Borough's bowling club, were on their way home.

Having completed a strenuous, lively but very enjoyable week touring the welcoming and rewarding clubs of the southern counties they were tired but victorious.

As always, every day had met with stiff, keen and determined opposition on the bowling greens and the ensuing lively tussles had led to a string of closely fought, competitive and rewarding wins for the visiting team.

Now, with five wins in five days the boys were on the way and looking forward to a restful and early return home.

Then of course there was the pleasure of watching the ladies' team turn out against the top county side of North Snodsham on Saturday.

Elated, the team had boarded their coach early at Brighton and after some excited chitter-chatter had settled down for a morning snooze, oblivious to the surroundings as the warmth and gentle vibration of the coach lulled them to a sleepful state.

Overhead the coach driver welcomed the passengers…

'Good morning ladies and gentlemen. My name is Tim. I am your driver for the day. Welcome to Valley Tours excursions.'

He paused for a second and then continued…

'Today we are delighted to be your guides on this wonderful sightseeing tour of Shakespeare country. We will be arriving in Stratford-upon-Avon in approximately five hours…'

Click!

The microphone switched off.

Undeterred, the team slumbered.

* * * *

Twenty-four ladies in their best whites relaxed in the clubhouse with tea and biscuits, whilst a slightly flustered Molly Coddle took charge of a manic and chaotic kitchen.

Meanwhile an apologetic county president sat quietly and discreetly in the bar area whilst Percy rang and rang until the phone could ring no more, as he tried to contact key players and representatives.

Doris 'Posh' Doolittle, the Lower South-Borough's ladies' captain, had arrived at the clubhouse in record time.

Still with freshly ironed white blouse untucked, hair unfettered and hat in hand, she arrived with a slightly wild look to her eyes and more than a hint of panic.

One large cup of strong coffee later a rather more level-headed Doris introduced herself to the equally prim Matilda Tinkleton and sat down to see what could be salvaged from the impending tour disaster.

Percy had managed to have some success with his multi-line 'Chris Tarrant style' phone-a-friend and a number of members had arrived in haste to assist, participate, or in Charlie's case, to hinder the madcap proceedings.

The Rt Hon. Ronald 'Squiffy' Regis, club president, abandoned golf on the 11th hole and arrived in plus-fours.

Douglas Doolittle MBE, vice chairman, had set aside his late breakfast and rushed over armed with his *Financial Times* supplement and a rasher of bacon.

Charles 'Charlie' Chesterford, Hon. secretary, always available for anything, more or less, nearly dropped everything in his haste to be on the scene with so many ladies!

Reginald Trimley Esq., the Hon. treasurer, was still on his way, but being a touch short-sighted could well be halfway to Manchester by now!

A number of others arrived in rapid succession.

Percy was soon joined by Patrick Albright, Bertie Tattleford and Tony 'Trigger' Havershall, who all turned up in quick order, after all, they had not needed to adjust their hair or repair make-up.

Doris's decimated ranks were soon replenished as the ladies began to arrive also.

Diane Ditherford entered the clubhouse in full swing, rabbiting as always about the weather, the lack of parking spaces and the price of baked beans at their local Co-op.

Cynthia rolled in quietly with a still warm and very imposing Victoria sandwich on an equally large plate.

Sheila 'Legs' Ramsbottom, all six foot two of her, strode confidently into the clubhouse in a slightly less than regulation pleated white skirt, and several cups of tea were immediately spilled by the gentlemen.

Phillippa joined the swelling numbers with young Abbey in tow; Pauline also, although somewhat stressed at having to abandon her rehearsal at the local playwright's society production of *Aladdin*.

Doris and Matilda had been debating hard for an hour or so, writing and rewriting lists, considering potential possibilities and formulating plans only to bin them and begin again.

Finally they arrived at a feasible solution, not necessarily the most sensible, in fact possibly one not covered by the rule books and certainly one guaranteed to be a 'first' for the bowling fraternity.

In fact it was probably going to make the national papers if a press representative ever got hold of the story.

Agreed on their decision the two captains stood up and, at a signal, the touring county president called the members for some quiet and their fullest attention.

'Order please.'

He was not heard over the babbling and chattering.

'Order!'

One or two stopped, but some were in full flow and Diana Ditherford in particular was a veritable torrent of waffling.

Sir John Jeremiah Tinkleton was used to getting order and his former career as a regimental Sergeant-Major left him with a very firm authoritative voice when time required it, and certainly this particular time was very appropriate.

He gathered wind into his lungs much like inflating a pair of bellows, opened his mouth and let rip.

'O-r-r-d-d-d-e-e-e-rrrr!'

Cynthia Cobblethwaite fainted clean away, lucky to be caught by the very well placed Charlie Chesterford.

One or two ladies screamed with fright, biscuits were lost in mid-dunk, a terrified Bertie Tattleford broke wind involuntarily and Sheila Ramsbottom's teacup violently jerked upwards in direct nervous response to the *en masse* expulsion of air occurring ten centimetres from her right ear.

She was unfortunately standing immediately behind Sir John and had no warning whatsoever and even more unfortunately her teacup was not empty.

A quantity of warm tea, white with two sugars, propelled by the cup's acceleration, arose from its launch pad and fell in slow motion onto her already too transparent previously white blouse, revealing a lot more than it should have.

Charlie turned rather red around the cheeks and considered that it was lucky that Sheila was of 'slight' build.

Apparently her favourite dress style was 'au natural'.

Tony wondered if perhaps she had rushed out from home just a bit too disorganised and unprepared.

Sir John pondered whether he'd shouted just a little too loudly.

Perhaps he did slightly overdo it.

He mused, but decided that at least it had had the desired effect as you could now hear a pin drop.

Sheila, normally one for brashness, boldness and tongue-in-cheek satire, turned a shade of deepening pink and disappeared to the ladies' room with a bar mat draped strategically over her bowling assets.

Bertie, pleading a silent innocence, opened a few windows and Charlie steered Cynthia towards the bar in search of a stiff drink.

The captains took the opportunity to regain the players' momentarily distracted attention and Matilda Tinkleton, grabbing the bull by the horns, metaphorically speaking, took centre stage.

'Ladies and gentlemen, if I could have your attention please.'

The members settled back down and faced the speaker.

'As you are all aware, there have been a few 'technical' complications with the arranged match between the ladies of Lower South-Borough and North Snodsham.'

She gave a fixed clinical stare at Sir John over the top of her glasses and he visibly withered into his armchair.

Matilda continued...

'We have however managed to come up with a feasible solution so that we may enjoy the day and the company in a spirit of good bowling.'

She paused for breath… and then carried on.

'16 ladies from North Snodsham are to be picked from our touring team and will then play 16 'ladies' from the Lower South-Borough members, in teams of four, on four rinks.'

Again she paused and then with a wry expression on her face added…

'Lower South-Borough, due to the short notice, have only eight ladies present.'

The Rt Hon. Ronald 'Squiffy' Regis politely interrupted…

'Er, excuse me, did you say eight?'

Doris Doolittle, ladies' captain, intervened…

'Yes. Our team will feature myself, Sheila, Cynthia, Diana, Phillippa, Pauline...'

She paused

'And... Miss Molly Coddle and Miss Abbey Doolittle.'

Squiffy spluttered into his tea.

Molly sat down in shock behind the kitchen, which would have been fine if there had still been a stool there to sit on.

The nearest she had ever been to a wood was in 1964 with little Bernie Bartum Jnr and that one had had bluebells in it!

Abbey stood in shock, jaw dropped, alongside her mum; after all she was only 11 years old and only played in the junior league.

Doris continued...

'Under the circumstances we have overlooked certain irregularities and eight of our men will partner our ladies to make up the numbers. The men will be Douglas, Percy, Bertie, Charlie, Reginald, Ronald, Patrick and Tony!'

It was Percy's turn to choke on his tea, being elevated from club reserve to tour team challenger was a mighty step even for a Reverend!

Reginald looked distinctly worried; he was more than a little bit short-sighted and already had problems viewing his computer spreadsheets.

Perhaps he could borrow a pair of binoculars from Dennis, or even a telescope, and then get someone to relay the fall of shot via his mobile phone.

Percy remained undaunted; he was in fact already relishing the challenge and the prospect of being able to rub shoulders with the cream of the crop from the visiting county.

The other men were already chattering amongst themselves and discussing tactics and team pairings when the captain spoke again.

'However...' she said.

There always seemed to be an IF or a BUT or a HOWEVER in any conversation which involved Doris and this obviously was not going to be an exception.

'However...' she repeated. 'Under the club rules all games must be balanced by the same number of players on each side.'

The men stared at each other…

They thought that Doris's point was blindingly obvious…

After all, one could hardly expect eight men to play against 16 women, no more then you could expect the opposite.

Reginald, albeit short-sighted, was very sharp on other matters, being an accountant, and his interpretation of all things gave him an edge in lateral thinking… he was already one step ahead of Doris.

Percy happened to glance across at Reginald and couldn't help but notice the ashen hue that glazed his countenance.

He began to have sudden uneasy misgivings and excited nervous apprehension, all at the same time, which was not easy to do whilst remaining impassive under the gimlet eye of Doris Doolittle.

Doris continued to orate, but in a manner rather unbecoming of her, with more than a hint of mirth playing around the corners of her mouth.

'As such, all gentlemen participating in the match will be required to participate as ladies…'

There was a stunned silence from the men's camp.

The ladies however were unable to contain their merriment and a titter of amusement spread like a Mexican wave through the masses.

Charlie piped up…

He had a habit of speaking up when he felt the need to, and he felt the need to right now.

'What exactly do you mean, participate as ladies?' he said.

On reflection, perhaps it wasn't the wisest of questions to ask, given the outcome that was to follow, but nevertheless Charlie asked it.

'Exactly that,' said Doris. 'You will be required to dress up as ladies and act with the decorum that the ladies show on the green, so no smoking and no swearing and absolutely no hanky-panky, Charlie Chesterford!'

Charlie was lost for words.

Percy wondered if it wasn't against his religion.

Douglas though it sounded rather kinky.

Bertie rather liked the idea!

Percy, after pondering, volunteered the second least wise question of the day…

'But where on earth are we going to get eight sets of ladies' bowling clothes?'

Doris looked round at Matilda who likewise turned towards her team.

'Ladies?' she said inquisitively.

The eight non-playing ladies of the North Snodsham bowling club stood up with big grins on their faces.

'Well,' said Doris, 'does that answer your question, Percy?'

The gentlemen were, to coin a phrase, backed into the corner, between a rock and a hard place, with nowhere to run, and they resigned themselves to the inevitable.

* * * *

Two hours later, the ladies' team of North Snodsham stood waiting on the green, four ladies on each of the four bowling rinks.

With each of the teams stood two of the Lower South-Borough ladies.

The rinks were all smartly set out with new mats, shiny cots, measuring sticks and scoreboards at the ready.

The captains, Doris and Matilda, stood in the centre of the green ready to announce the start of the game.

Only one thing was missing… the gentlemen.

'Come on gentlemen…' prompted Doris towards the changing rooms.

The other ladies took up the call.

'Yes, come on, chaps, let's be having you.'

'Game on, boys… hurry up.'

'Christmas will be here before you.'

In unison the combined voices of the amassed ladies' 'choir' of Lower South-Borough and North Snodsham burst into song…

'Why are we waiting?'

'Oh wh-y-y-y are we waiting?'

The changing room door creaked cautiously open…

Percy stepped out into the summer breeze, rather bashful, cutting a fine figure in a pleated white skirt and matching blouse, his blushes spared by a modest 32A-cup that hardly raised an eyebrow.

Douglas, vice chairman, followed cautiously behind.

Rather a tall and comfortably built guy, he seemed to be struggling in the longer pencil skirt which was quite obviously a size too small.

Ronald, president, had decided to 'play up' and make the most of his performance, so above his amply proportioned body he sported a fake perm hair-do with a purple rinse.

He had even gone to the trouble of tinting his handlebar moustache; there was no way he was going to shave it off so this seemed to be the next best thing.

His significantly hairy legs below the rather short skirt gave Ronald a rather odd appearance and one might have been excused for thinking King Kong had turned up as a transvestite.

Patrick was always keen to participate and entered into the spirit with a frivolity that was perhaps slightly overstated.

Certainly the much-padded 46DD-cup on his slim frame was! It was not hard to imagine that he would have serious problems with his eyesight when attempting to bowl.

Tony, being Tony, did what he always did best, and achieved the impossible and unimaginable.

Not being overly astute in the wonders of womanhood he stepped out with his bra on back to front and did an impromptu impersonation of the Hunchback of Notre Dame.

Perhaps he would have looked slightly less ridiculous if he had put his underwear on underneath and not on top of the blouse and skirt

Charlie, always the show-off, opted for fishnets.

Bertie was regarded as a bit of a 'loose cannon' with his volatile temperament, stubborn personality and liking for all things 'native'.

He had already caused consternation around the changing rooms following his revelation that he was a fully fledged member of the local naturist's club!

No one knew quite what to expect, which was just as well.

Bertie emerged from the changing rooms with an entrance that would have put Marilyn Monroe to shame. Indeed it could easily have been imagined that he was auditioning for the Moulin Rouge.

Wearing a 'figure hugging', fashionable, pleated two-piece with matching summer hat and a white feather boa, Bertie 'cut a dash'!

Percy looked closely and muttered a quick prayer; apparently Bertie had borrowed the make-up as well.

'My God, he's even shaved his legs!' exclaimed the astonished county president.

Bertie appeared to blush, beneath his blusher, mascara and glossy lipstick.

The door opened again noisily as the fine figure of Reginald Trimley burst forth into the limelight.

Reginald, short-sighted at the best of times, could see even less without his glasses...

Having coyly exchanged his 'proper' collar and tie for the more feminine bra and blouse, he was, whilst blushing furiously, struggling to cope with the wiles of feminine lingerie.

To put it another way, he was trying to put on a pair of ladies' tights whilst retaining his dignity and composure... Of course, men are well renowned for not being able to multi-task and the mystery of ladies' lingerie is not one to be tackled lightly.

With a mighty heave Reginald had raised the gathered folds of the tights over his knobbly knees rather too quickly...

His right foot burst through the sole of the fragile material as the elasticated hem accelerated upwards to chest level.

Reggie was in a panic, over-excited, over-balancing, and his glasses had fallen off into the tights.

The door beckoned and he fell.

Reginald Trimley's sudden appearance caught everyone's attention, indeed it could hardly have failed to.

Half naked, with an overstretched, overstressed pair of ladies' nylons adorning him from foot to neck, Reggie arrived with a bang and a crash!

Underneath, his pale blue Co-op Y-fronts, now surmounted by a pair of large framed spectacles, gave him the appearance of a blinkered bank robber in drag!

As one the ladies roared with laughter...

'Ha! Ha! Ha! Ha! Ha!'

'Oh dearie me... hee hee.'

The cheerful chortling increased exponentially as uncontrollable, unfettered, hysteria swept the ranks of the county's finest…

'Oh dear… Oh God… Ha! Ha! Ha!'

They tittered and tee hee'd and ha ha'd until tears ran down their faces and their legs could no longer hold them upright and they had to sit down quickly on the grass bank.

Sir John, for once totally overcome, became completely carried away and began rolling about the green chortling and guffawing hysterically until he rolled into the ditch and stopped suddenly.

He came to a standstill for two reasons.

The more obvious was, of course, that having arrived in the ditch there was really no further to roll.

Secondly, and less expected, but the reason for stopping, was the sudden confrontation, face to face, with two large, slightly bloodshot, maniacal eyes!

Sir John ceased laughing very abruptly as he tried to fathom, without comprehension, the meaning of the sudden apparition, literally whisker to whisker with his nose.

* * * *

The day had been a rather peaceful one for Rollo, the vicarage cat. After chasing a field mouse around the clubhouse for half an hour he had become rather tired, as cats do, and had sought a quiet, undisturbed place to nap.

A small ditch below the grass bank on the east side of the green offered the perfect place, sheltered from the breeze, with the warmth of the seasonal sun.

Rollo settled down, curled up and wrapped his very large 'loo brush' tail around his body.

His ears appeared just above the level of the ditch, much like an early warning radar station, twitching when some distant noise or voice disturbed his slumber.

He shivered when he heard the titter of young Timothy's voice.

His tummy trembled slightly when the teacup and saucer shattered on the ground.

One eyelid raised in a curious perplexed fashion when 'Little Tim' rose up the flagpole.

The background noise of comings and goings passed him by as nothing more than a vague and distant event.

He was dreaming merrily of big fat mice roasting on a spit at Christmas right up to the point at which Sir John called for 'ORDER' in the clubhouse.

The effect, although diminished by distance, still rippled like an earthquake across the green and Rollo woke very suddenly indeed.

Startled out of his dream by such a verbal outburst, his fur positively exploded in all directions as if someone had walked along with a cattle prod and shot 5000 volts through him.

Anyone looking in his direction at that time would have been bemused to witness the sudden appearance of a giant fur ball levitating two feet about the ditch line, stiff legs akimbo and eyes stretched fully open.

Rollo plunged to earth with a thud, a wide-eyed, rather dazed and bewildered, glazed expression passing across his battered countenance.

He looked around, then around again.

Silence reigned.

Round and round he turned, his ears peaked, whiskers twitching, nose quivering and an obvious startled expression, but not so much as a fly flew or a bee buzzed.

Seconds turned to minutes and Rollo began to settle, his loo brush impression subsided until he resembled much the same cat as he had been prior to the 'earthquake'.

The warmth of the sun began to tell and finally he settled to the ground, his paws crept forward then stretched slowly to their limits, his tail flexed and outward bound.

And so Rollo the vicarage cat slumbered peacefully through the morning... through lunch... and into the early afternoon.

The sudden arrival of 16 stone of uncontrolled hysterical county president 'en masse' was not really Rollo's idea of a subtle wake-up call.

It can only be said that Sir John was very lucky indeed that he didn't land directly on top of the cat, or indeed that Rollo's precious and highly sensitised tail was not squashed, flattened, damaged or otherwise impeded by his unannounced appearance.

THUD!

Sir John arrived...

Rollo stayed put, stunned into a state of frozen immobile shock; his eyes flared open until they resembled huge saucers with dark yolks floating wildly in the centre.

An equally shocked pair stared back.

Two pairs of bushy whiskers twitched and vibrated in unison.

A low pitched, throaty *'M...e...o...w!'* emerged from Rollo's gaping mouth, as, with lips pulled back, he accelerated quickly from sleep to full caterwauling in a loud crescendo matched only by the equally reticent cry of panic from Sir John.

In mutual harmony Sir John's plaintive cry, rose, much like that of a wailing baby, self perpetuating in key, tone and tenacity.

As Rollo, for the second time in one day, expanded like a hairy sponge ball in the early stages of *rigor mortis,* his front paw shot out at great speed.

With the image of razor-like talons emerging in close proximity, Sir John took off like a 'bat out of hell'.

He rose fully upright, leapt over the ditch and hit a breakneck speed of seven miles per hour in a fraction of a second, which was not bad for a gentleman of his considerable and portly build.

The haunting cry of a much maligned pussy rang in his ears like a broken record, un-abating as he roared across the green.

BUMP! THUMP! BUMP! THUD! THUMP!

The vicarage cat bounced along behind the runaway president much as if he was tied to Sir John by a piece of strong elastic.

John had been fast off the mark but not quite fast enough and Rollo's claws had latched on his right sock very firmly indeed.

THUMP! MEOW! BUMP! MEOW! THUD!

The hysterical laughter of the club ladies and cross-dressers, which had begun to ebb, now flowed again as they bore witness to the amazing double act of the 'dynamic duo'.

Rollo bounced... Sir John ran... and as his sock began finally to unravel, the cat became further detached and increasingly angrier.

Sir John disappeared around the clubhouse, with 13 feet of woollen strand and a very, very agitated cat in hot pursuit.

The large mass on the end of the strand didn't quite make it around the same side of the flagpole as Sir John...

Whirling around and around on a rapidly shortening strand, Rollo ascended the flag pole in spiralling fashion until he came to rest, dizzy, disorientated and disabled, in a fuzzy ball of fur and wool half way up its stem.

A while later, with the benefits of new socks, strong tea (with brandy) and a very large bowl of double cream, both Sir John and Rollo settled down to the refuge of the clubhouse, albeit at opposite ends.

The ladies' match was now in full swing and the two guests settled down to watch the antics.

Despite the unusual line-up the game was progressing at a great pace with much joviality and it was a good job no one had noticed the reporter from the local gazette standing nearby taking pictures.

He had arrived after a hot tip-off, which had nothing to do with Sir John being in close proximity to the club telephone.

The game was lengthy, competitive and closely fought until the last shot but later was to become a much talked about match in the annals of club history for its moments of sheer classic comedy.

After all, who could possibly forget the sight of…

Patrick, now a flamboyant 46DD, trying his best to bowl a 'firing' wood whilst blinded by the up thrust of his newly acquired buoyancy aids.

Bertie having a tantrum because he chipped his nail varnish on the grass as he bowled a wood.

Tony using the reversed bra cups to carry his spare woods between ends.

Douglas, in far too tight a skirt, bowling two handed, with legs akimbo like a squatting sumo wrestler.

Reginald trying to bowl one handed whilst holding his skirt down with the other, not wanting to display too much panty-hose.

Charlie, with shirt undone one button too far, score card tucked in fishnets, and the rear of his skirt unwittingly trapped in his belt after an energetically played shot, providing the player behind with a less than palatable view of all things.

Ronald, at a key moment of bowling, with his fake perm sliding down over his face, playing on blindly and despatching his bowl completely in the wrong direction, decapitating a rose, four tulips and the press photographer's sun-roof.

And of course, good old Percy, the unassuming, shy, out and out amateur bowler, all round nice guy and timid preacher.

Good old Percy…

Now, recorded for posterity, the first ever gender bending, cross-dressing, religious Reverend last seen flouncing up the bowling green, handbag swinging, singing falsetto style 'PRAISE THE LORD' as he played the winning shot.

Well done, Percy!

* * * *

Paul, David, Eric, Clifford, Jack, James, Bernard, Johnny, Dennis and Frenchie were still on their way home.

They had enjoyed the warmth and comfort of their luxury coach for several hours now and had slumbered throughout the journey.

Paul was the first to stir, one sleepy eye gradually opening as he subconsciously picked up the drone of the driver's voice on the tannoy.

He noticed, blearily, that there appeared to be a lot of large hills in the distance as he peered through the misted windows.

'Strange,' he thought, 'I can't remember there being too many hills around Lower South-Borough.'

The driver's mechanical voice resumed: 'Ladies and gentlemen, welcome to the last port of call; we will shortly be disembarking at Stratford!'

Paul woke up suddenly.......Stratford?

CHAPTER FOUR
JULY

THE CLUB'S
DAY OUT

The summer bowling season was never one to pass without mishap.

For many, especially those enjoying an early retirement, it was an excuse to escape the dull routine of home life such as the outstanding DIY jobs that had been steadily growing in quantity for a number of years.

One or two seized the advantage to severely thrash or otherwise humiliate a neighbour whom they couldn't stand, without any fear of legal retaliation.

With a few it became the only respite from their partner's constant nagging, moaning and griping now that they were no longer safe in the garden shed or pigeon loft.

To some it presented a golden opportunity to sit at a bar all day, enjoy free drinks from the younger players and idly chit-chat until the fuming wife appeared at the pavilion door with a plate of burnt offerings that was once a roast dinner.

For individuals it offered the chance to participate in a dating agency that guaranteed the other person always shared at least ONE interest!

With the ladies, it became a haven, a source of intelligent conversation with equals that didn't revolve around football, beer and pubs, but instead the more important issues of make-up, glossy magazines and retail shopping!

For the much older generation the club became 'home from home' where they claimed 'squatter's rights' to the most comfortable armchair in the warmest corner with the best view and easy access to the bar.

It was never a good idea to innocently return their warm smiles and their friendly beckoning gestures to come and join them in the equally inviting seat opposite.

There was almost an iron clad guarantee that their opening gambit would be 'Mine's the usual' or 'Make mine a double.'

Subsequently, you would find yourself returning from the bar a few pounds lighter, with the impromptu round, pork scratchings, dry roasted peanuts, cheese 'n' onion crisps and obligatory pack of Hamlet.

Of course then, having indulged the bowlers with their favourite tipples, and accepted the invitation to sit down nearby, they would feel duty bound to return the gesture, in a manner of speaking.

This was usually in a conversational trade off and usually began with the age-old tradition of 'During the war…'

For others it was the chance to shine, excel and compete in a sport they loved and a challenge on which they thrived; they were the bowlers.

There were however one or two dates special to all members and ex-patriots of the club; these social gatherings allowed all to share the camaraderie and good spirit (normally alcoholic) of each other's company without fear of being compromised.

These events included the annual ladies vs. gentlemen bowling competition for which each team competed enthusiastically to avoid getting the 'wooden spoon' for the worst performance.

Then of course there was the club finals day when the best of the best and sometimes, depending on the luck of the draw, the worst of the best, competed for the club silver, or in some cases plastic and glass

There still remained many other memorable occasions, however, one perhaps was the firm favourite…

One that every year was greeted initially as a 'good idea', gradually gained tangible doubt and scepticism as the day approached and often caused retribution and conflicting arguments long after the event had passed.

This was of course the club's 'Annual Day Out'.

* * * *

Tap.

Tap tap tap.

Tap tap tap tap tap!

Percy looked up.

Charlie, in his official role as club secretary, was in the process of posting a new and rather large, colourful chart to the club notice board.

'Hello, Charlie, what are you asking for volunteers for this time?'

Big Jim looked up with a bright look in his eye...

'Any alcoholic prizes?'

Bernard joined in with his tuppenceworth…

'I hope it involves ladies.'

Molly looked across from the relative safety of her kitchen, frowned at the men and tutted.

'Don't you men think about anything else apart from beer, bowls and chasing women?'

Bernard smiled broadly.

'Yes!' he said with a naughty expression on his face.

'Of course,' said Jack, 'There's wine and spirits too!' he beamed at Molly from the armchair.

Molly gave them a look of disgust, threw her rather damp kitchen cloth in their general direction and went about her regular routine, with one eye of course on the whereabouts of Bernard.

Bernard and Jack turned their attention back to the notice board.

'Well, come on then, Charlie, spill the beans, what's new?' piped up Percy from the relatively neutral zone of the bar area.

'It's the list for this year's annual outing,' said Charlie.

One or two other pairs of ears perked up around the clubhouse.

Bertie joined in with the first of several comments...

'Well, I hope it's better than that day out bird watching on the coast,' he said.

Apparently Bertie had had other birds on his mind when he signed up and was only cheered on arrival by noting the presence of a discreetly signposted naturists' colony in the vicinity.

'The fish and chip trip wasn't much better,' said Dennis.

Everybody had looked forward to a nice walk and then good old-fashioned fresh cooked fish and chips open-wrapped in newspaper and partaken of at the end of the local pier.

Nobody had mentioned that they would have to go aboard an antique trawler aptly named the *Mary Celeste*, brave almost gale-force conditions in a bitterly cold north-westerly and attempt to catch their own!

The ladies were definitely NOT impressed with the memory of trying to attach wriggly, smelly lugworms to hooks purpose made for the world's largest sharks whilst their hands were frozen like blocks of ice.

Molly shuddered at the memory of a still playful Bernard slipping a lively worm down the back of her summer dress.

Bernard hadn't thought it was that bad; it had, after all, only taken them 15 minutes to fish her out of the ice cold water after leaping overboard in shock.

Doris joined in the rambling commentary...

'The food had better be fresh this year,' she stated.

'And it had better be dead too!' as an afterthought.

Percy remembered that one: it was the coffee morning at the Civic Hall with the continental cuisine and an afternoon of bridge.

Doris had, for once, been quite enthusiastic and polite until Frenchie 'Wide Boy' Phillips had sidled up to her.

Being tired of her usual rejections of his advances and suggestions of a date he had pointed out that the delicious chicken leg she was nibbling was in fact a frog's leg and the rather large pistachio nuts she had munched away merrily at all morning were in fact the continental delicacy of caramelised baby snails.

'I didn't think much of those continental shellfish either,' muttered Tony. 'The insides were still raw and I broke a tooth as well.'

'They're called oysters,' interrupted Charlie, getting tired of all the commotion. 'They're meant to be like that. You're supposed to swallow the inside not chew the bloody thing,' he said, rather too sharply.

And then, as an afterthought, 'And you're not supposed to eat the shell either!'

Tap!!

Charlie hit the last pin in rather too hard... or would have done had he actually made connection with the pin in the first place.

Unfortunately for Charlie he was distracted with all the commotion and his eyes were in one place whilst his hammer wielding hand was in another.

The hammer successfully hit a pin, in fact the pin that held the cord that in turn held the notice board firmly fixed to the wall.

Only now it wasn't so firmly fixed... Charlie's hammer saw to that.

The weighty board descended southwards complete with pin and plaster, pausing *en route* to make contact with Charlie's foot as it reached ground level.

Sticky plasters have many uses and just a short while later they were in much evidence.

There was rather a large one around Charlie's toe.

Another even larger one supported the reinstated notice board, albeit temporarily.

A third encompassed Charlie's right thumb which had been just a bit too close to the offending pin when the hammer circumnavigated its circumference.

Charlie had retired to the bar area, as was tradition for all manner of spiritual uplifting, and he was being thoroughly spoilt by one or two of the ladies who had rushed to his aid.

Well, after all, he was a very wealthy widower and not bad looking in a roguish kind of way.

A large gathering of members were now excitedly discussing the source of Charlie's displeasure, not so much the pin or the hammer, but the notice board and its contents.

CLUB OUTING 2005, it read...

ADVENTURE WEEKEND FOR ALL AGES said the slogan emblazoned across a variety of tranquil and eye-catching photographs.

There were a number of events to participate in, all sounding attractive, sociable and suitable, with at least one interest for every member.

Perhaps, after all, this was one year when the club annual outing would be a success.

There were columns marked off for members to put their names up and a space to nominate a selection of activities in which they wished to participate, or at least sample.

Percy was casting his attentive eyes over the list of potential pastimes... the choice was numerous and varied and he rather hoped there would be plenty of time to try more than just one.

Already many had placed their names on the waiting list and Percy had no doubt that one or two had probably been volunteered without their knowledge.

He pondered over the list...

ANGLING LESSONS FOR THE NOVICE
Jack, Patrick, Colin, James

BIRD WATCHING FOR ENTHUSIASTS
Doris, Denis, Pauline, David

ACTIVITY TEAM SPORTS
Charlie, Tony, Frenchie, Johnny

SWIMMING WITH NATURE
Bertie, Molly, Phillippa

TREASURE HUNT ON WHEELS
Bernard, Reginald, Paul, Tommy

THE GREAT RIVER ADVENTURE
Clifford, Russell, Abbey, Timothy

MILITARY MEMORABILIA
Squiffy, Derek, Eric, Sheila

APOLOGIES FOR NOT BEING AVAILABLE
Diana, Cynthia

Everybody was required to choose at least one main activity and one reserve just in case there was an oversubscription of numbers.

Percy thought carefully and then, with discretion taking second place to valour, he selected 'the great river adventure' and 'swimming with nature', just to make the numbers up.

Charlie by now was quite plastered in more ways than one following the libations of alcoholic intake proffered by ladies keen, if not eager, to offer a soothing hand for his furrowed brow and even his toe.

'Well done, Pershy, old chap,' slurred Charlie from the comfort of his harem-surrounded soft seating, with a twinkle to his slightly blurred eyes...

'Don't forget to bring your wellish, camera and praysh book,' he concluded in a further aberration of the Queen's English.

Percy could be quite shrewd, uncannily so, in detecting people's hidden secrets and he could see that Charlie had one right now.

Even though Charlie's senses were rather dulled, the twinkle and the turned corner of his tightened lips gave a clear indication that something was up!

'What exactly do you mean, bring wellies, camera and prayer book?' inquired Percy, clearly offering the club secretary the opportunity to elaborate.

Charlie declined, but with a drunken snigger he said, 'Tthiss will be the bes-s-t club outing ever.'

'Hic!'

Then he fell over.

* * * *

As always time passed quickly and before the club members knew where they were it was the morning of this year's annual club outing.

Already a small coach stood idly in the club car park, the original minibus having to be replaced because of the number of members wishing to now attend this prestigious event.

It was a glorious July morning of the 22nd, and even at this early part of the day, 6.00 a.m., the sun was rising full in the sky, and the light shimmered through the heavily leaved trees spreading dappled shade and dancing rays of warmth wherever it fell.

Across the green scampered the full figure of Rollo, excessively vibrant, obviously in fine fettle, bouncing sideways stiff-legged back and forth across the turf before tearing away like a mad March hare only to race back again as something else caught his attention.

Anybody watching would have been rather surprised, and maybe even pleasantly delighted, to see the lighter side of Rollo as he pursued flies, leaves, gnats and rose petals with equal ardour and lunacy.

Rollo was in a world of his own and enjoying every moment. He was also a very clever and mischievous cat and he wasn't slow on the uptake that something else quite special was 'in the wind' today.

Clearly it was more than just a coincidence that Rollo was playing on the green at that particular time and on that particular day.

Back in the clubhouse the open doors invitingly welcomed the arriving members, and steam already rose from the urn almost merrily as a line of cups awaited the delivery of an early morning cup of tea.

There had of course been plenty of talk about the proposed day out, the participative events and the fun and thrills to be shared by all.

Jack was really looking forward to the prospects of a relaxing day by a tranquil lake, surrounded by woodland and wildlife, whiling away the hours fishing.

Of course his prospects of actually catching anything were likely to decrease *pro-rata* to his intake of 'medicinal' substances which were never far from his hip pocket.

But then one should always take precautions against the chill of the early morning air, shouldn't one. Not forgetting there was a chill in the lunchtime air and most definitely a distinct coolness in the afternoon air.

He arrived ready to go, with a telescopic rod and an ancient reel, attached to which was a length of line thick enough to moor the QE2 and sporting a float that would have probably taken the weight of the legendary vessel to pull it under.

Clearly Jack wasn't an up-to-date or experienced fisherman.

With a large floppy camouflage hat adorning his head, a matching Hawaiian shirt, Bermuda shorts and wellies, there was little doubt that any fish that wasn't blind would be at the other end of the lake to Jack.

Dennis couldn't help but snigger to himself as he witnessed the arrival of 'Big Jim'; after all, the mobile riot of colour much resembled a traffic light on legs, and he pondered on how anyone could dress so foolishly.

Dennis, also known to his friends as 'Sticky' because of his similarity in stature to a stick insect, emerged from the rear of his car.

His tall skinny frame was almost bowed down under the weight of equipment he carried; indeed he might well have been a member of an elite marine expeditionary force posted behind enemy lines for three months.

A large portable telescope and tripod were strapped at an angle across his groaning back, over which an enormous rucksack now perched.

There was a multitude of bird recognition books, waterproof identification charts, sketchpads, pens, pencils and brushes fighting for space alongside a flask, Mars Bar, packets of crisps and tin-foil wrapped spam sandwiches prepared freshly the night before.

Around his neck dangled several pairs of binoculars…

There was a positive array of ornithological weaponry: bifocal, tinted, auto focus, anti glare, high resolution, wide angle, short range, long distance, close vision, auto-zoom and digital enhancement, all encased in rubberised, latexed and armour plated cases.

And if the sheer scale of his anticipated bird watching assault wasn't enough to stun the feathered population into submission, his outfit certainly was.

'Sticky' was dressed head to toe in camouflage fatigues; hat, shirt, jacket, trousers, boots, all bore the multi-patchwork quilt effect of multiple splotches in all shades of green, grey, khaki and tan.

He was further adorned by a large sheet of netting, much like a sack of carrots, into which he had cunningly and lovingly sewn a large number of leaves, twigs and even the odd branch!

Over by the coach the local gazette reporter Jiggy 'Snapper' Jenkins could barely contain his excitement and he took notes as quickly as his podgy little hands could write them.

He took pictures…

He took LOTS of pictures!

He took pictures until the batteries in his camera positively glowed red hot from the rapid overuse.

'Snapper' had already become something of a local celebratory figure following his 'warts and all' revelations of the club's county tour match the previous month.

His headline, 'CROSS-DRESSING COUNTY COACH-FULL CATCHES CLUB COMMITTEE IN LINGERIE LATHER,' made for interesting reading amongst the local and not so local population.

Following the exposé and more than a few red faces, the club had gained something of a cult status with the press and there had been more than a few people calling up to apply for membership!

Indeed, following the day of publication the club applications had nearly quadrupled, although one or two of those applying definitely had alternative interests other than that of just bowling.

Rollo had been approached by national television to participate in an advert for OSCAR'S CAT FOOD, but had not yet replied due to lack of an agent.

So Rollo carried on frantically chasing imaginary leaves whilst the reporter, in a haphazard manner, snapped away merrily at every opportunity as it unveiled itself.

As the members continued to turn up in a disorderly fashion, Jiggy couldn't help but notice they bore a distinct similarity to animals boarding Noah's Ark, always appearing two by two.

Charlie and Tony were the next to arrive, although perhaps the term 'arrive' was a little bit of an overstatement in Charlie's case.

Whilst not exactly the brightest of people first thing in the morning, he had only the previous night stayed over at Squiffy's, who happened to live next door.

Joined by Big Jim, Shelia, Trigger, Frenchie, Bernard and Cynthia, they had whiled away the evening hours over a few bottles of port and a hand or two of bridge.

The liquor had flowed, the cards had been most favourable and the banter light-hearted. It was frivolous enough, although at times rather 'near the knuckle', which certainly brought out the ribald and rumbustious personality of Aussie girl Sheila 'Legs' Ramsbottom.

With a laugh that could have registered probably a seven or even an eight on the Richter scale, an ability to consume copious quantities of alcohol as if she was drinking lemonade, a never-ending stockpile of rowdy jokes and a capability of playing cards much like a Las Vegas dealer, she was quite the 'live-wire'.

After drinking everyone under the table, winning most of the rubbers at bridge, reducing everyone to comical hysterics and still capable of walking on her very shapely 'pins', she had headed off to bed leaving the others to compose themselves.

Charlie and Tony were quite obviously still composing!

Molly Coddle, never the most adventurous of people, arrived dressed, as a precaution, in her best 'safe' clothing.

After countless years surviving post-war evolution, drought, rock and roll, punk and, worst of all, men, she arrived safely at her 50th birthday still a spinster and having never been kissed.

She was indeed a well proportioned, fine figure of a woman, perfectly preserved and naturally attractive, but usually with her shapely physique well hidden beneath multitudinous layers of shapeless clothing on most occasions.

Today was no exception.

Molly arrived wearing her best flowery blouse, thickest grey long-sleeved cardigan, ankle-length pleated brown skirt revealing just a hint of woolly tights, flat walking shoes and her favourite multicoloured woolly hat.

Percy stared across and sighed…

He really would have to tell Molly about that tea cosy!

Snap!

Jiggy took another picture.

Still the members continued to arrive.

Bernard, Reginald, Paul and Tommy all appeared *en masse* in deep consultation regarding their plans for the ensuing treasure hunt.

The conversation seemed to revolve around How? Where? When? and What If?

Squiffy, Derek, Eric and Sheila were the last to turn-up.

The Rt Hon. Ronald 'Squiffy' Regis didn't just arrive, he made an entrance!

Dressed in his very best 'blues', every crease perfectly in line and place, shoes polished, brasses rubbed till they sparkled, medals rattling and tinkling, and regimental tie knotted 'just so', Squiffy marched into the club compound.

His newly waxed handlebar moustache glistened brightly in the morning sun and one couldn't help but think it would be a mistake for him to light up a cigar at any point during the day!

SNAP!

Jiggy snapped again.

All in all, he thought, this already had the makings of a fancy dress parade and when added to the chaos and fun of the adventure park that awaited there was bound to be a riot!

Jiggy had, as all good reporters should do, done his homework and having 'surfed the net' he was pretty damn sure that the club members didn't realise just what they'd let themselves in for…

Most certainly he wasn't going to tell them.

The coach driver meanwhile was busy making the final preparations and stowing the small hand luggage, whilst Squiffy 'rounded up the troops' from the 'mess hall'.

Stepping into the open doorway, Squiffy tucked his baton smartly under his left arm and issued his instructions in true military fashion.

'Fall in! Fall in! Get a move on you 'orrible lot, come on, smartly does it!'

Squiffy was not one to be ignored when in full flow and he was very much in flow right now.

Teacups well cleared away in record time, biscuit barrels tightly sealed, cutlery polished and the clubhouse left spick and span by the time the hot water had escaped down the kitchen sink plug hole.

Squiffy's bellowed orders also caught the ear of the coach driver, another retired military driver, causing him, as an instinctive reflex, to stand to attention rather too sharply, which was never a good thing to do when bending over in the coach locker boot.

THUMP!

He banged his head, quite obviously, cursed a few times under his breath, muttered and puttered and went off to the men's room to inspect the damage to his head.

Rollo, still prancing around the perimeters of the green, had begun circling nearer and nearer the coach, one eye on the fleeing bug he was pursuing and the other on the comings and goings in the car park.

The coach driver was definitely going...

Rollo's ears twitched...

His body shivered in anticipation.......

The bug-following pupil refocused and joined the other one in monitoring the situation over by the coach.

The coach driver was going... going... gone!

And Rollo diverted course in mid-stride, powering across the grass like a missile, leaping off the bank and catapulting his very large body in one fluid bounce onto the lowered boot lid of the coach...

B-O-I-N-G!

The well hinged, well sprung boot lid acted much like a trampoline and reacted accordingly to the arrival of Rollo's not too inconsiderable bulk.

He went from full acceleration to full rise in an instant...

B-O-I-N-G! B-O-I-N-G! B-O-I-N-G!

Laws of mass acceleration, body weight and gravity played their part effectively and even Rollo after one or two bounces began to slow down...

B-O-I-N-G!

The last bounce was clearly one bounce too many for the much abused coach lid, and compressing against its sprung hinges it slipped the locking hinge without warning.

Rollo was already dizzy and disorientated, he had been charging around the green for the best part of an hour, hyperactive, much like a whirling dervish.

He had accelerated horizontally a bit too quickly and his 'take off' from the grass bank had been slightly over-zealous... he hadn't planned to arrive on the coach lid from a height of 23 feet.

Now having been bounced up and down like a bungee jumper he was cross-eyed, cross-legged and VERY cross.

A final, slightly lesser bounce hinted that he was going to come to a stop and his sore bottom was very much hoping that would be the case.

For a split second Rollo came to a halt...

But only for a second before the response came from the boot lid, reacting like whiplash after an emergency stop, and he found himself catapulted into the spacious boot like a rag doll.

THUD!

He arrived head first into the pile of bird watching equipment, fishing gear and various, ladies, and men's items of apparel.

'M-e-e-o-w!'

The lid snapped firmly shut, trapping the last two inches of tail fur in its rubber seal.

The coach driver, arriving back soon after, looked around his vehicle in a perplexed manner.

Having examined his head for damage and finding nothing more than a rapidly developing painful bruise he had headed back to the parking lot.

As he turned the corner he could have sworn that he heard a very pitiful yowl from a very angry pussycat and wondered if perhaps someone had stood on its tail or even caught it in the coach door.

He gave the coach a quick 'once over' but found nothing and, as he looked up, he noted a procession of club members already approaching.

They seemed to be marching in an ordered two by two formation with a strange man in blue at the helm and a plump, balding, perspiring person festooned in cameras chasing up the rear.

The driver ignored the strange performance, kept his lips tightly pursed, fought back a rising smile and stood apprehensively by the coach door.

He resisted the temptation to whistle 'The animals went in two by two...' as the club members filed past him onto the coach.

Squiffy led the men and ladies of Lower South-Borough Bowling Club smartly onto the coach and re-arranged their seating arrangements to ensure they were all segregated by sex, height and clothing colour.

All was ready at last for the great day out.

The coach driver shut the doors, climbed into his seat and turned the key; the engine roared into life as if eager to transport the passengers to their impending doom.

Squiffy turned to face his fellow bowlers and with an excited wave of his raised left hand which clutched a well worn cassette he said, 'How about a nice sing-song to get us in the mood?'

A half-hearted cheer intermingled with more than a few groans rose from the ranks as memories returned of previous years with 'SONGS OF PRAISE', which at least the Reverend had enjoyed.

It was bound to be a slight improvement after all on the terrifying experience of 1998 when Squiffy had obviously had a mix-up in his daughters' nursery.

The resulting discordant strains of Pinky and Perky singing 'The Sound of Music' had much the same effect on his captive audience as if he had played *The Exorcist* on full colour wide-screen DVD.

Little Timothy piped up from the back, 'Can I put my tape on please?' in a pleading sort of way.

'Yes go on…' shouted one or two others encouragingly. After all, anything was better than two hours of Squiffy's favourite tunes.

Being president, Squiffy could sense a revolt in the rank and file, so not wishing to invite a popular uprising he capitulated with a forced smile.

'Come on then, lad, bring your tape up for the driver and we'll get under way…'

Tiny headed to the front, eagerly clutching his favourite cassette in his hand.

Percy glanced over as he walked past and got a very good look at the front cover, only a fleeting glance, but enough to register it as a picture resembling the birth of Satan from the fire-pits of Hell.

Percy groaned, began reciting the Lord's Prayer, and reached for his Bible and ear plugs.

Little Timothy arrived at the front of the coach, smiled sweetly and handed the tape to Squiffy.

It had to be said afterwards that it wasn't really Squiffy's fault; he did not, after all, have his reading glasses on and he had no idea at all that the volume level was set very high due to the driver's liking for all things operatic, especially Puccini.

He inserted the tape into the player, the play button lit up and the motors began to whirr…

The strains of a harmonious organ riff began to play and everyone in the coach looked up inquisitively.

It's not easy to describe exactly the impact of the next few seconds. Clearly the members were expecting some light sugary pop music, or at the very worst the greatest hits of the Spice Girls.

Tiny had said, in passing, that it was a compilation tape of his favourite tunes… so there should have been at least one or two they would like.

A sudden air-splitting, nerve jangling, bone jarring banshee-like howl of electric guitars filled the coach, closely followed by the thunderous roar of amplified drums on a never-ending roll.

Little Timothy bounced up and down on the back seat shrieking gleefully and playing 'air guitar' as the riotous tones of IRON MAIDEN rocked the framework.

The gathered ensemble were not ready, indeed not even primed, for the aural onslaught of the world's loudest rock band orating the dubious benefits of indulging in the 'devil's work'!

Visually the effect on the passengers was similar to that of having passed everyone through the scariest ghost train ever created, and already several pacemakers were frantically working overtime.

Shell-shocked, fingers strained and taut with nails digging into the chair arms, backbones rigidly pressed into the backs of their seats, the strapped-in members were not so much immobilised as mesmerised.

Molly Coddle's hair stood on end much like that of a punk rocker whilst Dennis Ditherford's skin drew back so tightly on his gaunt frame he now resembled a member of the living dead!

Doris screamed so loudly her false teeth fell out!

Sheila rather liked it!

She even considered joining in with little Timothy on the back seat for a spot of impromptu trampolining but wisely thought better of it.

The coach disappeared down the main road in a cloud of dust and exhaust fumes as Motorhead screamed the virtues of the 'ACE OF SPADES'.

One hour later a much more subdued coach arrived at its place of destination having restored order amid the chaos and reinstated 'Songs of Praise'.

Squiffy had managed to retract little Timothy's cassette from the player after about 10 minutes whilst the deafened coach driver had snaked down the winding roads with one hand on the wheel and the other banging at the dashboard violently and shouting rather rudely.

It was a very good job that his voice had been drowned out by the tape; otherwise the Reverend would have had to severely admonish him!

With teeth, hair do's and pacemakers now restored to their original state, a quick round of tea from the machine and a rich digestive had more or less settled everyone's frayed nerves.

Indeed many were smiling and talking openly; there were even a few cries of delight, sounding like excited teenagers, as the coach pulled into the visitors' car park.

WELCOME TO ADVENTURE WORLD

A cheerful young man with clipboard stood waiting by the main door in matching cap, polo shirt and shorts emblazoned with the Adventure World name and logo.

He stepped forward greeting them in a warm friendly manner with a gleaming white smile as the visitors descended from the coach.

One or two of the ladies couldn't help but admire his rather toned legs and tanned weathered looks.

Molly positively blushed!

'Good morning, ladies and gentlemen, welcome to Adventure World, my name is Joshua and I'm your party organiser for the day.'

He paused briefly for the group to settle, and then continued.

'All the arrangements are already made for you today; we've received the list of your chosen adventures from your club co-ordinator and we will allocate you with an appropriately coloured pass and guide map.'

The club members were now like excited school children and were getting more animated by the minute as nervous anticipation took effect.

'If you'd like to collect your ticket from me so that I can check your name against our list please,' he said in a firm voice which made Sheila tremble.

'He can collect my telephone number as well if he wants,' quipped Sheila, and then with a touch of mischievousness added...

'And he can check any other details as well!'

Sheila was never one to speak quietly or be backward in coming forward and more than a few members heard her comments, including Joshua who glanced across with a slight grin and a twinkle in his eye.

Sheila turned a very bright shade of red!

Joshua continued:

'Please check the colour of your ticket and follow the clearly marked, coloured signposts that will take you to the right part of the park world for your chosen adventure.'

And with that the ladies and gentlemen of Lower South-Borough Bowling Club stepped forward to sign in.

Jack, Patrick, Colin and James were all ready for their idealistic day of relaxation by the lakes and, of course, a spot of angling thrown in.

Doris, Denis, Pauline and David were very keen to get out in the wood and search out the wildlife.

Charlie, Tony, Frenchie and Johnny weren't quite sure what the activities would be but were positively sure they would be competitive and fun.

Bertie, Molly and Phillippa just wanted to swim and relax, although Bertie did seem to have other things on his mind!

Bernard, Reginald, Paul and Tommy were all fired up and eager to take on the treasure hunt challenge, neither wanting to finish in second place.

Clifford, Russell, Abbey, Timothy and Percy already imagined the simple pleasure of floating gently down the river and the delights of a picnic in a rowing boat.

Squiffy, Derek, Eric and Sheila were in full 'war games' mode, looking forward to the opportunity of scrutinising military memorabilia in the museum and perhaps even trying out some of the former hardware.

Sheila had always been a bit of a 'tomboy' with a liking for 'Big Boys' toys!

Maybe they'd even get to sit in the cockpit of a Spitfire or be taken for a ride in a captured Panzer tank.

All checked in, ready to go, the teams lined up, excited now, eager to be off, and the air was full of gossip, nervous chit-chat and charged expectancy.

The coach driver approached.

'I'm just going to lock the coach up for the day now,' he said, 'but I'll just be in the canteen here if anyone needs anything or arrives back early.'

And with that he turned the handle to the luggage compartment.

The lid dropped open and he peered into the inky darkness, readjusting his eyes for a second after the bright sunshine of the morning.

It appeared to be somewhat of a mess inside: rucksacks, binoculars, tripods, fishing rods and thermos flasks lay everywhere.

The driver stared.

Two very large eyes stared back!

The driver blinked.

The large eyes just stared and got larger!

Rollo had been bumped by binoculars, bounced by back doors, bashed by bags, prodded and poked by poles, and half strangled by straps for an hour and he had had enough.

His nine lives had been thoroughly tried and tested in the last few months and they were getting very ragged around the edges.

His temper, already frayed back in April, was now fractured and frazzled and, not to put too fine a point on it, was stretched thinner than a piece of cling film!

It was hardly surprising that Rollo took off like a greyhound out of a starting gate and he took full advantage of the now absent hatch to charge forward through the wreckage like a thundering rhino.

BO-I-NG!

With a crashing leap that used the much stressed hatch door as a springboard, Rollo soared over the coach driver's right shoulder and charged across the open car park at full pelt, the dust rising behind his frantically clawing claws.

The first part of Rollo's plan worked fine in that he used the right exit, the door stayed open, he gained escape velocity and missed running into the wide-eyed driver.

He had not however banked on the accrued and cumbersome attachments following him like a line of empty cans on a wedding car.

CRASH! CLATTER! CLANG! BANG! CLATTER!

Rollo therefore careered across the car park adorned with a multitudinous variety of fishing tackle, binocular cases, handbags and even a complete rucksack, trailing thermos flasks and sandwiches in his wake…

The gathered members watched with looks of shock and disbelief as the maniacal cat charged around and around the parking area in ever decreasing circles before purging himself of the unwanted décor that now trailed halfway across the tarmac.

It was altogether far too much entertainment in too short a time for the onlookers.

As one the bowling ensemble burst into titters.

It rolled like a tidal wave of infectious laughter through their ranks until several of the members were in rampant hysteria, tears running down their faces as they watched the animated antics of the mischievous cat.

He was at last getting a taste of his own medicine.

Rollo may have been enraged, incensed even, at the turn of events that had otherwise ruined his well planned and executed escape from the club grounds.

Indeed he might have even responded to the joviality and mercilessness teasing of the bowlers had he not been more concerned about the comings and goings of the mobile car boot behind him.

Whilst he was no doubt preoccupied with freeing his limbs from the pursuing appendages he nevertheless took note of, and deep rooted offence at, the carry-ons and made a mental note to redress the balance at a later date.

Rollo, although a cat, also had a memory like an elephant, and his eyes and ears picked up every comment, every sound and every voice.

Clearly he anticipated a rewarding retribution not too far in the distant future.

He vanished into the shrubbery, finally free of the jettisoned luggage and shielded from the echoes of the ribald, riotous hilarity of the massed members.

He slunk off in a particularly foul mood, his much relieved tail trailing between his tired legs.

Having restored some sense of sanity to the proceedings, Squiffy started the Lower South-Borough members on their way to their organised events with a few words of good cheer...

'Good luck everyone! Watch out for the crocodiles. Last one back buys the drinks!'

Well, he never was one for big speeches, comedy wisecracks or adventurous conversation. Nevertheless the members took his words in good part, and with a spring in their step they all walked off down the pathways to seek out and enjoy the pleasure of their leisure.

Bertie led the ladies Molly and Phillippa down the winding woodland path.

Molly felt a little bit uncomfortable and awkward being almost alone with Bertie, who was, to say the least, an outspoken, almost cocky sales rep who wouldn't think twice about selling sand to a Saudi Arabian and would probably make quite a profit into the bargain.

No wonder, she reflected, he was known for his notoriety; she smiled at her own little joke, thankful that at least Phillippa was here; after all, she was quite a handful, being a strict, stern and forthright councillor.

Molly was getting rather warm under all her multi-layered apparel and, throwing caution to the wind, it wasn't too long before the shy spinster had whipped off her tea cosy and loosened the top button of her cardigan!

'Here we are, ladies,' shouted Bertie gleefully as they turned the corner and their eyes fell upon the most peaceful, idyllic, tranquil, natural haven it was ever possible to imagine.

The river opened into a large shallow bay, shaded by several mature willows in which a kingfisher rested with one eye watchful on the water below as the sun's warm rays cast a dappled mix of light and shade across the surface.

A gentle breeze wafted through the woodland as bulrushes and teasels swayed merrily by the newly build jetty that sloped easily and gently into the water.

Nearby three or four timber chalets stood on sturdy legs above the ground and at first glance the facilities looked to be absolutely perfect.

'These must be the changing and leisure facilities,' said Phillippa.

She climbed the steps towards the open doorway for a closer inspection whilst Molly waited nervously at the bottom.

'Superb!' shouted Phillippa gazing inward...

'There's a fitted kitchen, spa bath, barbeque on the patio, a fabulous view, even an artist's easel, and lots of fresh food, fruit and drink as well,' she exclaimed...

That's as far as she got in her recital of the much appreciated and well laden benefits of the visitors' chalet in front of her.

'Never mind that, ladies,' shouted Bertie, 'Let's get in the water!' and with that he rushed by the chalet heading towards the riverbank.

'Wait for us,' called Phillippa after Bertie's back as he tore past.

'B-b-b-ut we haven't g-g-got our cossies on yet,' stammered Molly...

Bertie laughed in a madcap fashion, long and heartily.

'Never mind that, ladies,' as he tore off his shirt and threw it over his shoulder...

'Life's too short!' as he kicked off his sandals...

'Last one in is a sissy!' as he undid the belt on his trousers.

Phillippa looked on aghast as Bertie's trousers dropped to the floor revealing a pair of brightly coloured yellow and orange Bermuda shorts covered in large green dots.

Molly blushed furiously and hid her face behind her tea cosy, although, for once in her sheltered life, she was not too shy to peek coyly through the spout hole.

Bertie looked over his shoulder, laughed loudly and dropped his shorts.

Phillippa fainted with shock as the white cheeks of Bertie's bottom bounced across the grass and disappeared into the water accompanied by a loud splash and a scream of pleasurable delight from the late-in-life naturist.

Molly still looked on as Bertie's bottie disappeared under the surface, and unabashed for once in her life, the shy spinster turned away with a twinkle in her eye.

So that's what a man look likes without his clothes on, she mused...

Good job he didn't run into the water backwards.

Molly sniggered at her wild imagination and decided that there must be something in the woodland air; she turned and stepped lightly up to the chalet where Phillippa still lay groaning.

* * * *

Bernard and Reginald followed closely behind Paul and Tommy as they stepped smartly along the well rutted woodland path, eager to get their own Adventure World experience under way.

It was definitely a case of 'Best Man Wins' in the age-old ritual of juniors vs. seniors and a treasure hunt was just the thing to do the job.

A treasure hunt on wheels was even better, pondered Bernard, probably mountain bikes, maybe even a tandem.

Whatever the case, with he and Reginald being keen cyclists and of course with Reggie's numeric and calculus skills they were bound to have the edge.

They turned the corner... and came to an abrupt halt.

Another smartly dressed Adventure World guide stood patiently waiting by a small parking lot, clipboard under his arm, and an expectant smile on his face.

Sitting side by side in the park stood eight very large, gleaming, 4 x 4, cross-country quad bikes.

They looked almost like V6 engines mounted on tractor tyres with bucket seats strapped on.

Paul and Tommy stood still with eyes wide open and jaws dropped.

'Wick-ed!' shouted Paul

'Wow... cool!' agreed Tommy.

Bernard and Reggie stared at each in disbelief and then, in unison, agreed the obvious in shocked quiet voices,

'Oh my God!'

* * * *

Doris, Denis, Pauline and David were not faring much better.

Festooned and encumbered by the mass of bird watching paraphernalia that would have been sufficient to kit out most of the RSPB membership of East Anglia, they had positively crawled along the footpath.

It hadn't helped that Dennis insisted on stopping every few seconds to respond to every bird call, feather sighting or pile of droppings.

Intent on pursuing a particularly interesting sighting, Dennis had charged into the brush in his camouflage netting and, without considering the outcome of straying off the permissive pathway, the others had followed in quick pursuit.

Fifteen minutes and much massed foliage later they arrived at the inevitable conclusion that they were thoroughly disorientated and totally lost.

Dennis was oblivious to his surroundings and the consequences thereof; festooned in his netting he was busy zooming in on the mysterious bird with his high-resolution long-distance auto-zoom Zeiss monocular.

CLICK!

'Got-cha!' he shouted with an elated scream, sure of his photographic capture of a rare passerine recorded for posterity in digital Technicolor.

Overhead the 'rare passerine' took off from its leafy perch with a rather plaintive call of alarm and Dennis couldn't help but notice its similarity to a chaffinch.

He stared closely at the miniature view screen... and pressed the zoom button.

It WAS a chaffinch!

The other members were by now all trotting off merrily to their individual leisure pursuits.

In particular the age-old military rivals Squiffy and Derek were now intensely excited; in fact they had probably registered about 'DEF CON 3' on the nuclear scale.

They were looking forward with great delight to the long awaited opportunity of re-enacting all the strategic events of previous wars dating back, no doubt, to Napoleon Bonaparte, with, of course, their own personal interpretation.

Squiffy, a retired squadron commander, always took the *aerial* overview, and saw himself as a self-confessed strategist *extraordinaire* who could have outmanoeuvred Eisenhower with his eyes shut and one hand tied behind his back.

Derek, a former desert rat, was more used to cunning and guile at ground level, but the heat of the sun had long been held responsible for his short temper and many members joked that 'he must have had his humour cells fried along with the sausages'.

When it came to any discussion about the War, and it inevitably became a discussion about the War when Squiffy and Derek met at the bar, then there always developed two completely alternative ends to any campaign, both opposite and extreme, and with an outcome totally different to the actual event.

Of course there was never any way that their views could be put to the test, or their theories put into practice, although the idea had been raised that perhaps they should take up computer lessons and participate in 'role play' computer games.

Today, at least, they would have the opportunity to reminisce over memorabilia, and spend pleasurable, if somewhat opposing, hours debating, cogitating and re-enacting days of old.

They turned the final corner into a large park over which a curved sign bore the legend CAMP EISENHOWER.

Squiffy couldn't help but notice that the entrance was flanked by two sentry boxes and sandbagged machine gun posts, beyond which a line of grey buildings fully resembled those of a World War II American military encampment.

Even the authentic smell of burnt wood, old soot, oil and exhaust fumes tainted the surrounding air and a smoggy haze appeared to overhang the encampment as it lay deep in the shadow of the thick woodland.

Nice touch, thought Derek, as he breathed in the memory and vision.

'Welcome, ladies and gentlemen, to Camp Eisenhower!'

The sudden voice startled them both out of their deep thoughtful states as a smartly turned out and apparently senior member of the American military service stepped out of the sentry box nearest to them with a big smile.

'Welcome,' he repeated.

'This encampment is an exact reproduction of a traditional World War II military camp in which you are free to roam at your leisure. You will find barracks, a working canteen serving victuals as it would have been, our military museum, training grounds, even a re-enactment of the conditions during the blitz!'

He paused briefly for them to digest the information, and then continued.

'Further more you will find in the vehicle compound a number of genuine military hardware pieces, which you are free to examine at your leisure. You will also discover in the first hut a range of service uniforms to make your visit realistic and more memorable. Please feel free to change into any of these and enjoy your day.'

With that the 'officer' stood sharply to attention, saluted and quick stepped back into the sentry box, no doubt to renew his acquaintance with a hot mug of coffee whilst he awaited the next visitors.

Squiffy and Derek positively beamed with delight and after thanking the 'officer' profusely they clipped on their visitors' name tags and marched briskly, side by side, into the compound.

Eric was already in his element but Sheila was beginning to have some doubt about being alone in the barracks with the 'Three Wise Men'.

Twenty minutes later Brigadier 'BIG BANG' Derek Dunstable stepped in a sprightly fashion onto the adjoining veranda in a set of freshly laundered camouflage fatigues bearing the rank and insignia of the desert rats. His left chest bore much evidence of many successful campaigns witnessed by row upon row of brightly coloured military ribbons.

He was almost immediately joined by the Air Marshall 'BOOM BOOM' Ronald 'Squiffy' Regis, equally and impressively turned out in RAF blues 'n' twos with every crease in matched perfection.

Eric soon found a suitable authentic pilot's outfit complete with helmet and emerged as if he were ready to lead the Dam Busters into action.

Sheila was the last to arrive but made the most impact.

It was the legs that done it!

Kitted out smartly in a Women's Auxiliary uniform with a crisp white shirt, jacket, tie and a long pleated skirt, it was certainly agreed by the others that she had a lovely set of 'pins', especially in those stockings!

Derek turned to his comrade in arms.

'Shall we?' he inquired.

'Yes, let's!' said Ronald.

Together they stepped purposefully towards the vehicle compound.

Sheila and Eric fell into step behind them.

* * * *

Percy was thoroughly enjoying his day out.

Free of the confines of his strict religious requirements, he now walked happy and light at foot, alongside Clifford, Russell, Abbey and Timothy.

The children stepped happily and eagerly side by side, with the lightweight picnic basket swinging easily between their outstretched arms.

Percy was already dreaming of the lazy sun-kissed sally down the river on the deck of a small boat, or maybe even an old fashioned raft, gently bobbing in the light turbulence as the waters bubbled over small rocks creating eddies in the flow.

Today was the most perfect of days, he thought to himself, as his ears picked up the sound of water gently lapping on a rocky edge just around the corner.

He picked up the pace and the children, sensing his eagerness, likewise speeded up and together they raced around the corner.

'Wow!' shouted the children in unison.

'Oh my, how delightful,' exclaimed Percy.

Clifford and Russell, following close behind, just had to agree.

A stunning open-bayed lake lay before their eyes, a large log cabin with veranda perched on its edge, as water lapped and splashed and sparkled around the stony margins.

The obligatory Adventure World representative stood waiting with the statutory clipboard and white toothy smile.

Percy was pleased to note that the guide already wore a flotation belt as a firm indication of the company's safety-conscious customer programme.

He couldn't help thinking that the portly figure of Russell Cobblethwaite, their most senior member, might need two flotation belts or possibly even three.

Percy glanced across expectantly to the line of stout, low lying, timber rowing boats by the jetty as the guide formally welcomed them.

'Good morning all, it's a glorious day, a nice breeze building and plenty of rainfall yesterday so we should get plenty of flow.'

Percy wondered why 'flow' was so important for a lazy day on the river.

'The water temperature's a pleasant 22ºC, not that we want anyone to fall in,' beamed the guide. Well, if you're all ready, let's get aboard. Please pick up your lifebelts, waterproofs and safety harnesses from the raftsman on the way in.'

Harness? thought Percy, why on earth do we need a harness?

Most certainly they wouldn't need waterproofs for a day's boating.

After all the conditions were quite placid and no more than a light spray lifted from the lake's surface.

He pondered further...

Raft?

The guide had definitely said raft, R-A-F-T, not boat, not yacht, not dinghy, but raft...

Percy was somewhat confused and now just a slight bit perturbed.

'Hello, what's that?' exclaimed the guide, spotting the large wicker basket held by the children.

'It's our picnic,' piped up Abbey.

'Oh, you won't have time for that,' said the guide...

'You had better leave it at reception and you can all enjoy it after you get back from the ride!'

Abbey and Timothy did as they were told, placed the hamper alongside the veranda near the lodge entrance and followed Percy, Russell and Clifford around the corner to the lake... where everyone had come to a complete halt and all were standing wide-eyed and open jawed, staring at the water's edge.

It WAS a raft, of that there could be no doubt, not a luxurious, comfortable sailing yacht with an air-conditioned cabin and chilled champagne, but a replica of *Kon-Tiki* ready to take on the Pacific ocean. The stout timber craft was constructed of massive sturdy-looking logs, mounted criss-cross, four deep in a reinforced 20-foot square with heavy rope rigging running around its perimeter on stanchions.

A dozen streamlined and robust padded bucket seats were bolted to the framework at even distances.

Clifford was the first to utter a remark.

'Isn't that a bit over the top for a day out on the lakes?'

One of the boat crew, in the process of strapping on waterproofs, paused and looked up at Clifford, with a large toothy grin.

'Well, it would be if we were just going for a gentle sail,' he laughed loudly and lively-like... 'but you are definitely going to need this where we're going.'

Clifford decided to feign ignorance and thought that perhaps the crew were just following health and safety requirements so it was wise not to question them further.

'Come on, everyone, let's get on board then. This looks like a lot of fun,' said Clifford, with a forced cheerful smile, as he decided to take the initiative, as all good councillors should do.

And with that he stepped boldly out onto the raft!

It was, surprisingly, very stable, and didn't move so much as an inch as he walked across it nervously towards an empty seat.

'Look, everyone, this is fine!' he exclaimed and proceeded to jump up and down enthusiastically.

The raft continued to remain stationary, with not so much as a ripple in the water to indicate Clifford's antics.

Percy and Russell looked visibly relieved and the colour began to settle back into their drained faces.

Abbey and Timothy were very excited!

They were, after all, typical of teenagers and didn't know the meaning of fear.

The children were already stepping out onto the raft expectantly, so Percy and Russell, not wanting to look frightened or silly, did likewise.

Moments later Percy could simply not believe what all the fuss had been about.

The raft was indeed so stable he hadn't even noticed the change from *terra firma* and he smiled broadly, partly out of relief and partly with renewed anticipation.

This was after all going to be a glorious outing on the lake, and with all fears and doubts banished he was rekindling his desire for a wonderful day ahead.

Soon the party were firmly strapped in, harnesses attached, waterproofs on and in good cheer they even began to break into a discordant rendition of Cliff Richard's 'Summer Holiday'.

With everyone aboard, the guide slipped the hawser ropes from the jetty and gave the raft a punt with a large wooden pole allowing it to gain steerage way in the natural current.

Fifteen minutes later the ungainly looking structure, now firmly caught in the current, was bobbing gracefully and moving purposefully across the lake under the guidance of the crew member at the steering rudder.

'Having fun yet, Reverend?' shouted Clifford from the other side of the raft.

'I haven't had so much fun since meeting Mrs Cobblethwaite in the air raid shelter,' interjected Russell.

Percy gathered a deep breath to answer back, but from the corner of his eye he noticed that the water was definitely getting a little choppier, with white flecked spumes of spray now lapping over the timber edges.

'Well I... er... er...'

The stout frame had begun to pitch and buck just a little now and Percy began to feel uneasy.

'Well, you see...' stuttered Percy...

But that's really as far as he got before his brain registered the fact that the lake had narrowed quite considerably.

In fact, so much so, that they seemed to be gathering speed and were now moving forward much more rapidly towards what appeared to be a wild looking area of churning water topped by white wave crests crashing against rocks, and it was starting to get noisier too.

Percy called over to the man at the rudder, whilst gesticulating wildly with his outstretched arm…

'Is everything all right?'

The guide looked back with a beaming smile…

'Surely it shouldn't be as rough as that,' shouted Percy 'not just for a raft ride?'

The guide grinned again and shouted back, 'Well you did book for white water rafting!'

All too late Percy remembered the warning from the inebriated Charlie and it was perhaps a benefit to all that the noise of the water hid the mixture of expletives that emerged from the Reverend's lips and which would later require quite a few '*Hail Marys*' and maybe even a trip to a confession box.

Percy looked aghast at Clifford and Russell as they plunged full tilt into the seething raging mass of white water.

Together, as one, they opened their mouths wide and screamed at the tops of their voices…

'A-a-a-a-r-r-r-g-h-h!'

The wooden platform kicked like a bucking bronco as it met the rapids head on and the three older members hung on for dear life; the nearest crew member could have sworn that Percy was leading them in a recital of 'The Charge of the Light Brigade.'

Abbey and Timothy were having the time of their lives, whooping and cheering and singing and enjoying the cacophony of madness as spray threw up into the air and descended upon them in great crashing waves.

It wasn't long however before Percy's knuckles and even his face had drained completely white, to match the water, as the raft pitched and swayed and nosedived and spun and thundered its way down the man-made gorge.

At one point the platform raised high in the air on an enormous wave crest and Percy made the mistake of opening his tightly shut eyes just for a second, just in time to see the impending 'roller-coaster' drop over a miniature waterfall!

He screwed his eyes tight and went back to his prayer recitals with renewed fervour!

Thirty minutes and five miles later they arrived, intact, at the end of the elongated millrace and floated gracefully off the last eddies into an open bay.

The raft drifted sluggishly towards the tree-lined banks as Percy muttered a final prayer, Clifford put away his hip flask and Russell turned down his pacemaker.

The children continued to whoop and holler unabated, overwhelmed by the excitement and intensity of the whole experience.

Everyone was wet, totally, completely, utterly soaked, and Percy was sure that they would never dry out again; it rather reminded him of a day out in April and he shuddered from the memory.

He couldn't help but notice, as he mused through his befuddled thoughts, that what seemed to be the rear end of a white hippopotamus was drifting serenely past the raft.

Bertie's naked bottom floated by the astonished on-lookers, as he gave them a cheerful wave.

'Hello Percy!' he exclaimed, rolling over and waving with one hand.

Percy quickly covered the children's eyes.

He couldn't help but think that the whole world had gone slightly mad.

An ear-splitting scream filled his ears and he was shaken abruptly out of his dazed state by a 'Tarzan-like' call of the wild.

Percy looked on in total uncomprehending amazement as Molly Coddle swung down through the trees on a large rope, let go in mid air and somersaulted with a huge splash into the water alongside Bertie.

Percy couldn't help but notice that Molly was still wearing her tea cosy, but apparently little else of note.

Beyond the cascading water he observed that a plumpish figure appeared to be running along the jetty in a small pink thong and bikini top.

It leapt off the sprung plank at the end and catapulted into the air arms and legs akimbo, screaming with apparent pleasure…

'W-h-o-o-p-e-e-e!'

The scream of pleasure became one of shock and anguish as the buxom shape took on an identifiable form just as it reached the peak of the take-off and saw the figures on the raft for the very first time.

'Oh my G—-o—-d!'

Phillippa Spindleforth, former posh councillor, screamed loudly in realisation as she plunged before the onlookers' eyes into the water with a huge splash!

'Not quite,' said Percy, smiling rather reverently, 'just one of his servants.'

A pink bikini top floated to the top of the water adjacent to Phillippa's point of entry.

At that point, one could be forgiven for thinking that this comedy of errors had aptly drawn to a close.

Certainly Percy did, having endured the unexpected insanity of the white water rafting, the shock of Bertie's bare bottom, not to mention the unbelievable encounter with Molly's streaking and the councillor's animated watery antics, he simply did not consider the likelihood of anything else developing.

But then he hadn't allowed for the fact that other members were still absent from the carry-ons.

The tally of those yet unaccounted for reduced in number with the arrival of several stressed, tired and clearly frustrated bowlers in camouflage netting, with binoculars focused and cameras clicking, seeking the whereabouts of a rather large 'parrot' with an unusual mating call.

Molly at that point, with tea cosy still very much the only item hiding her dignity above water level, took a discreet paddle around to the very rear of the raft, where Bertie likewise had sought refuge and the use of a spare waterproof jacket.

It was perhaps unfortunate for all concerned that the camera clicking also was much in evidence from the local gazette reporter, Jiggy 'Snapper' Jenkins, who always made a habit of being in the right place at the right time for the perfect scoop.

Percy raised a weary hand to acknowledge the presence of Doris, Dennis, Pauline and David, not really comprehending the rising roar of a full throttled engine approaching at pace from the woodland adjacent to the jetty.

* * * *

At a top speed of 30 miles per hour the 16-ton heavily armoured 'dreadnought' tank could make quite an impression!

It had been sitting quite harmlessly in the military compound 15 minutes ago whilst Derek tried out the driver's seat, Squiffy checked out the ordnance and Eric played with the radio.

It was much like being back in a children's playroom as Eric 'called in' fake bearings, Squiffy 'zoomed in' the hardware on imaginary targets and Derek added the sound effects of a racing diesel engine.

'Vroom vroom.'

'Blue leader to control, target sited.'

'Vroom vroom.'

'Engaging the enemy.'

'Vroom vroom!'

'Open fire as the target bears!'

The 'children' were having lots and lots of fun!

'V-r-o-o-o-o-m-m-m!'

Brigadier 'BIG BANG' Derek Dunstable froze in mid-call, aware that the last 'vroom' had definitely not come from his lips but from the large engine nearby!

Air Marshall 'BOOM BOOM' Ronald 'Squiffy' Regis, none the wiser, continued to engage the enemy and had used his fervent imagination to throw in a few aerial targets as well.

Eric appeared to have lost the plot as he was talking to Napoleon and had just called for reinforcements from the Praetorian Guard!

To be fair, it wasn't really Derek's fault.

Ever the tomboy, Sheila had joined the proceedings, mounting the tank turret and attempting to slide her remarkably long legs through the inspection hatch which was a tad too small for her shapely assets.

She wriggled and jiggled and swore!

Already halfway committed, she was carried forward by her own momentum and it wasn't long before her stocking-covered pins were 'on inspection' all the way up to her thighs as her skirt became jammed in the hatch combing.

She wriggled some more, thrashing her long legs about, in the process knocking Eric off his perch and colliding with a number of buttons, levers and switches, one of which just happened to be the starter!

V-R-O-O-O-O-M-M-M!

With Derek's hands already manipulating the track controls and his feet pumping the clutch control pedals he had no chance to react to the engine's activation; the throaty roar of the massive machine rose to a crescendo and it lurched backward suddenly!

Derek kicked out wildly, catching the wrong pedals, and the tank charged forward like a rampaging buffalo as it gained full traction, careering across the compound in a cloud of dust.

Sheila was evicted from the turret like a pea popped from a pod, and, from his perch deep inside, a very dizzy Squiffy hung on for dear life as the turret spun around and around like an autogyro; Eric was already heading for the escape hatch!

* * * *

Percy's hand almost reached halfway toward a weary wave before the tank arrived, and arrive it did in spectacular fashion.

The goliath burst through the tree line and charged down the track at high speed in a dust storm of its own making.

Percy could make out the terrified figure of Derek at the controls, and a goggled Eric clinging to the hatchway of its revolving turret.

As the gun rotated through 360 degrees the unmistakeable figure of Sheila 'Legs' Ramsbottom came into view screaming loudly; she was mounted on the gun like a rider in the saddle, both hands hanging on to the barrel for dear life, legs rigidly thrust outwards and her skirt billowing like a hot-air balloon.

Percy blushed and thought it prudent to avert his eyes.

The tank mounted the jetty being the next natural impediment in its progress and thundered along the straining length, leaving a line of broken timbers in its path until the jetty ran out.

Unfortunately the tank didn't.

They were never designed to fly and this one certainly wasn't about to alter history, but it nevertheless left the woodwork with a fine impression of one attempting to do so...

Engine racing, the metal monstrosity tore into the air for all of three seconds and then plunged towards the water with a huge, resonating, thunderous bellow.

SP-L—L—A—-A—-A—-A—S—S—H!

Everyone on the raft hung on for dear life as the leviathan impacted with the pool.

In a cloud of roaring steam as the engine flooded, it stopped immediately, sending a tidal wave of water racing up the shoreline, which receded almost as vigorously it had arrived, leaving behind a trail of debris including a drenched bird-watching party, a semi-clad Sheila, butt-naked Bertie, Molly in a very soggy and overstretched tea cosy and a very shocked looking topless councillor.

Absolute silence fell as all of the members and guides looked on in stunned amazement at the scene that lay before them.

CLICK!

A rather excited Jiggy 'Snapper' Jenkins clung precariously to his perch high up in the tree and snapped away. He could already see a Pulitzer Prize heading his way.

Percy groaned.

* * * *

It was perhaps two hours later that a very subdued group of bowlers in a multitudinous array of mismatched clothing arrived back at the car park to partake of the previously arranged fish 'n' chip supper at the Adventure Park canteen.

Luckily a plentiful supply of tea and coffee had been on hand and a number of concerned park representatives were readily available to sort out the required needs of the members.

As they arrived, a small group of exhausted, but apparently very content, men headed towards them; they were covered head to foot in multicoloured paint!

Oblivious to the other 'goings on', Charlie, Tony, Frenchie and Johnny joined the others with big grins sported on their otherwise paint-splattered persons.

'Activity team sports?' enquired Percy.

'Paint balling,' came the sighed reply from the tired but happy bowlers.

They looked over the ramshackle appearance of the other members of Percy's motley gathering and asked the patently obvious question...

'So how was your day?'

Percy sighed deeply, despairingly and sat down.

* * * *

Over in the bushes a bemused, bedraggled cat eyed the people warily, his attention momentarily distracted from the pink thong he had been playing with.

CHAPTER FIVE
AUGUST
THE FESTIVAL OF BOWLS

The events of the previous month were almost forgotten, and the revelations from the newspaper coverage finally dwindled to nothing more than a few lines on an inner back page of the sporting column of the local gazette.

The initial coverage from the local paper had been picked up by Anglia Television and Jiggy Jenkins had sold his exclusive pictures to an eager tabloid for an undisclosed six-figure sum resulting in the club members' antics being splashed across six pages of *The Sun* newspaper.

Sheila riding the tank made front page whilst Molly Coddle without her tea cosy ended up displaying her attributes in full colour across page three.

Needless to say a rash of threatening letters from members' solicitors ensured a healthy 'donation' to the club's coffers by Jiggy Jenkins.

Molly became the overnight 'pin-up' girl for the 'OVER 50 AND SINGLE' gentlemen's club of Great Britain and a substantial offer from 'PENTHOUSE PIN-UPS' was rumoured to have been made to Molly, which she hadn't yet turned down.

There was rumour of a Hollywood-style National Lampoon movie being made in much the same vein as *THE FULL MONTY* and the title of *CARRY ON PERCY* had already been bandied about.

The influx of money from the pictures, donations, sponsorship deals and other lucrative offers had already funded fully half the costs of a new indoor bowling centre for the club.

Meanwhile, a certain 'councillor', trying to revitalise her career in the aftermath of the slightly exposed public image, was pushing hard for a matching grant from the National Lottery.

Membership applications for the following season had soared and B&B bookings in the immediate area had rocketed likewise as Lower South-Borough gained overnight celebrity status as a tourist attraction.

There was no doubt in the committee's mind that every day next season would be attended by a full house of visitors keen to watch the game, buy souvenirs, drink tea and dunk biscuits all day.

All in all, despite the initial shock to the system, the notoriety had after all been very beneficial to the club and only the other day they had received a number of sponsorship proposals, one of which came from the management of 'ADVENTURE WORLD'.

Evidentially the damage to the park had been superficial, but the publicity had been so great that their weekend breaks were sold out for the next five years.

Charlie, having been tipped off in advance and already seen the early morning edition of the newspapers, had mysteriously 'taken an extended vacation' for health reasons, to allow members time to cool off.

In the end, despite immediate calls to lynch him and leave him dangling from the oak tree on the village green, most members had been pacified and eventually forgiven him as the benefits of his little escapade had begun to pour in.

One or two things would never be the same again, of course.

Molly Coddle had suddenly become the focus of attention for the ladies' committee and hardly a day went by without her getting an invite to attend a local tea dance, Women's Institute meeting, statue unveiling or ribbon cutting at a new residential club.

She had, it seemed, gained cult status.

It stood to reason that, although still the shy and innocent tea lady at heart, Molly's eyes had been somewhat opened and it wasn't long before her revelations also led to a lot of interest in Bertie Tattleford and more than a few complimentary comments about his anatomy!

Derek and Squiffy had been contracted to write a monthly column, 'ALTERNATIVE MANOEUVRING FOR BEGINNERS,' for a well respected military magazine.

Percy's personal involvement with Lower South-Borough had not gone unnoticed at higher levels and this, combined with a popular appeal that was packing houses for his Sunday sermons and evening masses had caught the eye of the bishop.

There was rumour of a promotion, an elevation to a higher status for the Reverend.

Sheila found herself adopted by the Suffolk Regiment as the squaddies' favourite pin-up, and her tank ride had made her almost as popular to the older generation as Vera Lynn.

Apart from all the excitement arising from the club's now legendary day out, August saw be the hosting of another very, very important event on the Lower South-Borough social calendar, indeed the cumulative peak of the season's bowling.

Here, then, was the icing on the cake, the annual bowls festival! This massive event combined the end of the summer season's bowling with the club's singles 'finals' and a bowling tournament, an event open to all and sundry for which there was the not unseemly attraction of a very substantial cash prize of £5000.

There was of course a number of sponsorship bonuses which meant that the finalists could be enjoying the delightful pleasure of gaining a free weekend break, dinner for two at a plush restaurant, maybe a case of wine from a famous village brewery or even a year's supply of wild bird food from the local conservation centre.

So this event then became the 'Graceland' of bowling, the 'Mecca', the 'Holy Grail', a golden chalice, not often poisoned, to which all bowlers gathered like bees to a honey pot.

This year especially would be a year to remember, it was a 'Jubilee' year for the club, a double celebration to boot.

With Lower South-Borough celebrating 50 years since its creation, it was also the retirement year of their outgoing president, the Rt Hon. Ronald 'Squiffy' Regis, after five years as the club figurehead as well as being a former founder member.

Fifty golden years!

Yes, this year would be a very special year!

Well, needless to say, the applications were snapped up as soon as they were printed; in fact there was a waiting list of many club members from all over the region.

Invitations had also been sent far and wide and a list of luminary guests had accepted with much delight.

Quite probably, all of them would turn up with at least small digital cameras in their pockets and some might even have their own publicity agents in tow.

After all, they were never likely to miss a photo opportunity and one thing Lower South-Borough was renowned for in recent times was providing outstanding publicity!

It was set to be a prestigious event with well established and even infamous bowlers booked for the festival; indeed there were notable and reputable players from the England team turning up.

Even local hero Martin King was coming to the games!

Martin always took his games very, very seriously and, being a gamekeeper by trade, he was not someone to take lightly; indeed it would be unwise to say anything that might upset him.

In a match that was likely to produce a close run result he had been known to stand his shotgun carry-case near the bowling rink not necessarily to intimidate the other player, but 'just in case of rabbits' he would say.

A bowler would have to be wary of taking the lead and would be well advised to keep one eye looking over his shoulder; if Martin took to polishing his barrels as well as his woods then it could be a good idea to let him win one or two shots.

Spectators were well aware of Martin's tendencies; being a strong and robustly built Norfolk man, he was not backward in coming forward when a 'cannonball' style of bowl was required.

Indeed, in a competition only last year on the Britannia green on Great Yarmouth sea front he had enthralled the audience with his dexterity and skills.

He had launched a 'firing' shot that had not only scattered every previously bowled wood to the four corners of the green but had also dislodged two of the steel railings on the surrounding fence, careered through the timber-built café shack and impacted in the deckchair attendant's sandcastle.

All in all, this was truly set to be the most exciting and best attended event ever in the club's ancient history, and with the rumour of a 'royal visit in the offing it seemed that Squiffy's 'retirement' would be marked in classic style.

Percy sighed.

He did a lot of sighing, and this season in particular he seemed to have done an awful lot, well, that and of course the administration of copious quantities of sticking plaster, mainly due to the carry-ons of Rollo the vicarage cat.

Percy paused...

The cat?

Now there was a thing!

Since the events of the previous month Rollo had become ever more conspicuously absent from the vicarage snug where he had often whiled away the warm evenings on Percy's old cloak.

It had been Percy's best, velvet trimmed, quilted and lined and hand stitched, which he kept for special occasions such as weddings and christenings.

However, Rollo had taken a liking for it one day and had claimed ownership, which is the policy of all cats when they discover something they like.

What began as a friendly, even funny, contest of willpower began one evening with Rollo in playful mode leaping onto the trailing edge of the cloak as Percy walked past deep in thought whilst studying a new response for the forthcoming Sunday service.

Rollo had been dragged around quite happily for nearly two and a half hours and had even had time to curl up and feign sleep before Percy had realized the new acquisition.

This had developed over numerous weeks into a daily game and eventually a kind of mutual animosity with Rollo hanging on for dear life, claws embedded in the lining as Percy stamped around the vicarage trying to dislodge the furry invader.

Eventually Rollo won the day and the cloak had disappeared a few days later only to materialize, after a week's absence, in the warmest spot in the vicarage and covered in a dense mat of dislodged cat hair.

Percy had surrendered to the inevitable and bought himself a new cloak.

Which brought Percy back to the point of his meanderings…

He had noticed that Rollo was a much less frequent visitor to the warmth and security of his humble dwelling recently and even the lure of best tuna in jelly, his favourite, had not been enough to entice him in for a lengthy stay.

Percy had the distinct and awful feeling that perhaps Rollo was up to no good, and with the Festival of Bowls well under way every day had been one of nervous and concerned anticipation.

So far so good: five days had passed in glorious sunshine, good competition and great response to the variety of raffles, prize draws, secondhand book sale, cake stalls and other members' contributions.

The church benevolent fund was doing very nicely and Percy could see that the harvest festival this year should provide enough to reach the funds target for the redecoration of the recently restored church vestry.

For once the weather had been kind to the festival and five whole days of glorious sunshine had given them the golden opportunity to clear most of the bar stock including, against Percy's advice, the two barrels of Guinness left over from the previous year, which had, for reasons unknown, remained locked away in Big Jim's storage locker until its recent discovery.

A rather red-faced Jim was not so much embarrassed at the discovery, more disappointed that he should be deprived of copious quantities of best Irish draught to lighten his winter's solitude.

Nevertheless the reclaimed barrels had been sold at even greater profit and surprisingly no more than ten per cent of the drinkers had actually complained of queasy or upset tummies.

Sheila's bout of acute diarrhoea was being attributed to the spam sandwiches that she had left in the hot sun for three hours whilst she played in a competition.

Spam really doesn't respond too well to 180 minutes at 32ºC!

But no one mentioned the fact that Sheila had consumed 12 pints of liquid refreshment the previous night and, taking into account the fact that Charlie had been serving behind the bar, it could be 'taken as read' that the substance imbibed by Sheila had not been Coca Cola.

Percy sighed again.

It seemed it was the role of Reverends to do a lot of sighing when it came to looking after their parishioners, and certainly his congregation was one of challenge and diverse occupation.

He paused to drop the day's mail into the postbox outside the vicarage and turned wearily homeward.

Time for cocoa and bed, he thought, an early night would set the mind at rest and prepare him for the big weekend ahead.

Saturday loomed on the horizon and with it the biggest day of the season; Percy felt a little shiver of excitement quiver its way down his tense back.

Such a big day!

Such an important day!

Probably the biggest in the club's history!

He decided that perhaps, just for safety, discretion should be the better part of valour and he locked Rollo securely in the vestry for the weekend.

Percy reached the front door, turned the handle and stepped inside; it really was time for bed!

* * * *

Joe 'Dodger' Stubbs was slightly the worse for wear, and his condition wasn't improving but deteriorating rapidly in the failing light.

The area representative from FLASH HARRY PROMOTIONS hadn't got off to a good start…

As a local media company, in fact the only local media company, they had been engaged to organise the publicity and key events for the finals day of the Lower South-Borough Bowls Festival.

Joe was supposed to collect all the sponsors' gifts and prizes from the respective businesses and set up all the display banners around the green for the grand final.

His day began with a flat battery, closely followed by an equally flat tyre on the M25, a broken windscreen on the A14 and 17 miles of road-works on the A12 behind two tractors, a caravan and Old Ma Hubbard towing a wardrobe on a skateboard at 12 miles per hour.

It was already 8.00 p.m. by the time he arrived at the delivery yard of WILD ABOUT BIRDS, his last port of call prior to arriving at the festival grounds.

His van was already full of banners, boxes of bread rolls, picnic tables, a giant teddy bear, six kegs of best bitter, a case of whisky, the largest bar of chocolate he had ever seen, assorted cases of deluxe biscuits, giant jigsaw puzzles and even a bathroom kit.

Joe checked his list, and then checked it again.

He was supposed to pick up a year's supply of wild bird feed and a feeding station as a presentation for the Lower South-Borough Nature Gardens, where, he supposed, all the posh visitors sat, supped Earl Grey tea or Pimms, nibbled *petit fours* and talked 'LAH-DE-DAH' with a little finger crooked in the air.

Joe didn't go by the nickname of 'Dodger' for nothing, and years of 'bunking off' school had left him a touch naive in the ways of the world and its delightful mannerisms.

In fact the rep. didn't have the slightest idea what a feeder station looked like and whilst he fancied the thought that it was a small table around which wild birds sat with miniature knives and forks and small bowls of muesli, he thought it extremely unlikely.

Looking around the courtyard he could see nothing that remotely resembled a station of any description nor could he see a stack of bird food in bags.

Joe was never the brightest of people, otherwise he would have noticed that the large speed ramp he had driven over by the gate was indeed the feed stack and his large van was sitting quite happily parked on top of it!

Tired, hungry and extremely late, he was not in the mood to hang about or carry out a search of the entire courtyard in the dark.

He must take something back, he mused, and looked around desperately for something that looked remotely 'birdie' orientated.

His eye caught sight of a large construction arising from the flowerbed in the front garden.

It was a bird table, of that there could be no doubt.

But WHAT a bird table…

It stood fully 10 foot high, with a fine timbered roof perched over a cavernous feeding area that seemed, in the dark, to be the size of a car parking space.

There appeared to be a number of mini-shelves stepped at intervals down the main support post and it was festooned with an array of feeding tubes, fat-balls, peanut holders and even a water bath of some sort hanging from a high vantage point.

Joe supposed that if he looked closely enough he would find it had a small chimney, net curtains, painted flower pots and even a post-box outside the main door.

He made his decision and marched resolutely towards the construction, rolling up his shirt sleeves in a purposeful fashion to reveal large muscular biceps and a tattoo of Popeye.

Twenty minutes later a muddy, dishevelled, wild-eyed and bedraggled Dodger sat behind the steering wheel of his battered Transit, trying to peer around the array of bird feeders that dangled over the edge of his windscreen.

Inevitably, he resorted to fastening the monstrosity to his roof rack. Panting, grunting, red faced and all, he had clambered onto the roof hauling the table up after him.

He would have to worry about the large dents in the van later, he mused.

Anyone passing WILD ABOUT BIRDS at that stage would have thought that a demonic Santa Claus had arrived three months early and was trying to hang a Transit van off their Christmas tree.

Covered in a multitude of scratches and abrasions, splinters where splinters shouldn't be, bird seed down his Y-fronts and a fat-ball hanging from his cauliflower ear, Joe prayed he wouldn't bump into any of the local constabulary on their evening prowl.

* * * *

Joe had been waiting at the main gate to the bowling green for nearly half an hour.

The rep. had not been able to get an answer from the house next door and was beyond the level of rational reasoning.

He had given up on the idea of having a quick smoke when the local moth population took a liking to the glowing tip and began congregating like mosquitoes to a warm body.

Buzzed constantly by the neighbourhood bat, and squawked at in ear-splitting tones by the resident owl that just happened to roost in the treetop by the entrance, Joe was reaching breaking point and was decidedly jumpy.

He hated to admit it, but he was afraid of the dark!

Sitting in the van waiting for inspiration was never a good idea at 11 o'clock at night, especially at the end of a long wooded track in the country...

Even more so, when a plentiful supply of 'Dutch courage' resided nearby in a cardboard box on the passenger seat.

Joe deliberated and considered and, all things being equal, resisted the temptation to have a quick nip of the good stuff for at least 14 seconds.

Fifteen seconds later a rather more soothed, internally lubricated and warmer area representative sat on the van step with a capped bottle of malt whisky in his left hand.

Time and half a bottle of Scotland's finest soon passed, side by side, as a rather bleary-eyed Dodger decided to make an executive decision for the first time in his life.

Whatever it took, he was going to complete the delivery, even if he had to cut down the gate with a chainsaw!

The fact that he didn't even have a chainsaw had nothing at all to do with it!

He walked over to the offending gate and gave it a hearty kick!

Having kicked the tree, he shook his head to clear the alcoholic film that smothered him like a warm blanket and, in a moment of brief clarity, succeeded second time around in kicking the gate.

The hefty five-bar timber gate swung open easily on its well oiled hinges and clattered into the locking clamp.

It hadn't been locked at all, only shut!

Joe muttered and puttered under his breath, breathed deeply and went back to collect the van.

At that point it really would have been a disaster for the local policeman to cycle past and Dodger would have been in big BIG trouble.

Luckily for him one no one appeared...

Unluckily for him, he reversed back through the gate a little too fast, careered wildly through the car park and lodged the van a little too firmly in the prize petunias.

Joe, applying the brakes a touch too sharply at the last moment, succeeded in scattering pea gravel in every direction and excavating two linear holes in the surface deep enough to be classified as ditches.

A very shaken, but emotionally immune, inebriated promotions representative stood knee deep in battered bushes, pulverised petunias, cock-eyed cornflowers and lop-sided lupins and contemplated the carnage.

It looked slightly better than it was by moonlight, and even better through the alcoholic haze, therefore Joe decided to stick to the plan and carry on regardless.

Joe took the best part of an hour clambering up and down the grass banks with the promotional banners from the various companies sponsoring the festival.

It was a blessing in disguise that he still managed to remember that the banners were to be erected at the top of the bank and not on the green.

He even managed to stand all the boxes of prizes, food, drink, biscuits and other delightful goodies in a not too precarious stack by one of the clubhouse doors.

Admittedly it was the toilet door, but beggars can't be choosers, as they say, and a door is a door as much as a port is a port in any storm.

He could have sworn, on occasion, that a very shaggy apparition seemed to be stalking him through the light ground mist that tinted the darkness with its white woolliness, but he put it down to the effects of the alcohol and his own fears of the dark.

It was two o'clock in the morning before an exhausted, battered, bruised and shattered 'Dodger' staggered back to the van; the whisky bottle was much at its lowest ebb at this stage but at least the job was done...

Joe spotted the bird table on top of the roof rack!

'Oh hell,' he cursed, not too quietly or politely; he had forgotten all about that!

It took him another 20 minutes before he managed to retrieve the table from the roof, during which time he only fell off the van twice, and the new dent in the bonnet wasn't too bad, he felt, well, not as bad as the broken wing mirror when he dropped the table.

He peered into the dark void surrounding the van...

Now where was he supposed to put the bloody thing?

* * * *

The Reverend Percival Peabody awoke bright and early after a good night's rest, yawned widely, broke into a big smile and stretched his arms high over his head.

Percy could already see the bright sunshine streaming through the slightly ajar curtains and knew that it must be a glorious day outside, one which would bring only the finest bowling, best camaraderie and biggest sales in the raffle.

It was at last the day of the grand finals of The Festival of Bowls and a day that was bound to be full of thrills, spills, surprises and even a tear or two of happiness if all went to plan.

With a spring in his step, Percy positively leapt from his warm bed, determined to get a quick start; he had, after all, a lot to take care of today and he wanted to make sure that all was as it should be and no surprises awaited.

He looked in on the vestry just to make sure Rollo was still fast asleep on his best cloak and wasn't short of water or tasty titbits...

However, the warm wrap was empty and a tell-tale trail of claw-like tear marks in the vestry curtain led up towards the top window that Percy had left open for ventilation.

It appeared that Rollo had made good his escape.

A slightly more nervous Percy washed, changed and headed towards the vicarage door, with a slice of toast and jam in one hand and an almost empty cup of tea in the other.

He felt the urge to get to the club early, just to be on the safe side; after all, it never harmed to be ahead of schedule, did it?

* * * *

Percy dismounted from his new pushbike, removed his cycle clips, and pushed the gleaming new three-speed cycle towards the club entrance.

A whip-round from the club members had resulted in the presentation of a new vehicular transport for Percy, for which he was most grateful and much taken aback.

Indeed it almost brought a tear to his eye, especially when he sat on the new tough leather saddle for the very first time.

Finished in smart metallic blue and gleaming from all new parts, a carry rack over the rear wheel and a new wicker basket to the front, it was the best present Percy had ever received…

It even had rain guards and dynamo-driven front and back lights in case he chose to continue his pursuit of the Devil into the hours of darkness.

Almost immediately Percy noted that the main gate was open, and concluded that, even at this early hour, someone was already at the club and attending to the day's preparations.

He wheeled his cycle into the car park and did a quick 'recce' of the surrounding green.

Everything looked as it should be.

There was a large stack of deliveries near the clubhouse...

Those must be the raffle prizes and supplies for the kitchen, he mused quietly to himself.

The sponsors' banners were arranged around the green as they should be, although it did appear that some were upside down, two were back to front, and the Wild About Birds display was peeking out from the rose bed at a jaunty angle.

'Oh well,' Percy thought, 'that should take no more than a few minutes to put right, surely.'

His eyes scanned further around the green, taking everything into account in a fraction of a second, without his brain really registering the facts.

'Yes,' he thought, 'that's fine... there's a giant bird table in the middle of the green, a large white Transit in the lupins and a pair of bright pink socks dangling out of the far ditch.'

Percy turned away with a warm, almost serene smile and a distant look in his eyes as he busily ran through the list of things he had to do in the next three hours before the players began to arrive.

The penny dropped.

Well, actually so many pennies dropped that the noise could have woken half of the county and he could have been picking up loose change for the next three weeks!

Pink socks?

Transit van?

Bird table?

Percy began to feel very weak at the knees and did a slow, steady retake of the situation...

In the middle of the green there stood a towering timber construction that resembled a wild bird *a' la carte* trolley with a roof on and it was swarming with a wide variety of birdlife who simply couldn't believe their hungry eyes.

Usually it wasn't possible even to fly over the green without catching the beady-eyed stare of the green keeper; indeed it wasn't unknown for Patrick 'Postie' Albright to pursue pigeons across the green with a large empty bucket just in case they pooed in mid-flight.

To coin an expression, they were making hay as the sun shone.

There were birds on the feeders, fat-balls, peanut baskets and bird table, and even a pair of collared doves splashing merrily in the bird bath.

Nearby a wild-eyed, over-excited and anticipatory Rollo padded and paced around the lupins mewing and drooling with excitement.

Beyond the green there stood the white Transit van parked awkwardly on the edge of the car park with the rear part planted in the flowerbed, door open and showing some signs of distress; actually it looked like a herd of elephants had trampled up the bonnet and across the roof top.

There also appeared to be a trail of bread rolls from the side door leading down the pathway.

Percy was beginning to feel quite unwell and the colour began to drain from his already pasty face as he continued his visual survey of the carnage...

'Pink socks?'

'What on earth were a pair of pink socks doing on the ditch embankment?' thought Percy.

He paced across the green as an angry feeling began to rise inside and he surmised that he would probably need to say a few *'Hail Marys'* very shortly and maybe even make a trip to the Bishops office.

The scene gradually unfolded before him, the nearer he got to the offending articles of clothing, and the picture really wasn't that attractive.

The pink socks had legs attached to them and the legs were attached to the upside-down form of a large, unshaven, scruffily dressed man.

His tie was half-way around his neck under a torn collar, the garish shirt was missing a few buttons, revealing a string vest strained over an obese belly. There was a fat-ball dangling from one ear and he looked like he had spent the evening in a boxing ring with Mike Tyson.

There was also an empty whisky bottle resting nearby on the green.

Percy couldn't help but notice that the awful socks were in need of darning as a large pink toe was very visible peeking out like a large juicy worm... there was never a blackbird around when you needed one, was there!

A sharp gleam of annoyance crept into Percy's eye, matching the rather unusual feeling of what could only be called extreme irritation that he could feel inside.

Percy never, never, never got angry, but he was certainly heading in that general direction right now.

He spied the large steel bucket on top of the embankment.

The bucket was standing near a coiled hosepipe and a standing tap which 'Postie' used for the sprinkler system and garden flowerbeds.

Percy turned on the tap, and slid the bucket's rim under the nozzle.

The water was ice cold at the best of times, the night air had been rather cool and it was enough to make even the vicar gasp as his fingers passed under the tap.

Perhaps the sound of the water rushing into the empty bucket and drumming on the metal sides reached deep into the inebriated subconscious of Mr Stubbs, because he emitted a faint groan, his eyes twitched in a bleary fashion and the pink toe wiggled...

'A-r-r-r-r-r-r-r-r-r-h-h-h-h-h!'

The groan became an instantaneous scream of absolute fright as Percy tipped the bucket of VERY cold water over Dodger's head.

The rather gross figure of Joe Stubbs first staggered then lurched to his feet in an overhung, underdressed and very soggy fashion, and it was a good thing that none of the ladies were present: quite a few would have fainted and certainly Dodger would have given the ugly alien in any monster movie a run for its money.

'Urrrgh! whoos whash urggh oooh urrgh!'

Dodger groaned incomprehensibly.

'Oh gawd... whash the matterr urrgh?'

He opened his eyes and tried to focus on the apparition marching toward him, shook his head from side to side, rubbed his bloodshot eyes with his gnarled fists and finally recognized the approaching figure as apparently human and vicar-like.

'Oh no! Nooooooooooooooo!'

Percy advanced on Mr Stubbs with a grim look of determination on his face and turned on the hosepipe...

* * * *

It was just over an hour later, approaching 7.30 a.m. when Percy's 'cry of help' to the local committee had begun to pay off.

Patrick not so much arrived at the clubhouse as 'landed', in fact he left his house so quickly he arrived before his wife, and she was driving the car!

Squiffy, with the least distance to travel, made a diplomatic entrance and arrived last, as one should do when living next door!

Sticky Ditherford, for once, didn't dither but made haste; he arrived at the clubhouse with a trailer load of garden implements, a veritable shedful of tools and a good sturdy tow-rope.

Percy already had a good idea where he wanted to stick one of the garden forks!

Fortunately for Mr Stubbs he was otherwise engaged talking to the local constable.

Unfortunately, the local constable was engaged to Sheila 'Legs' Ramsbottom and had a strong liking for bowling.

Sheila was appearing in the ladies' finals later that day and it was clear that Sheila's fiancé was not overly impressed with Mr Stubbs.

The ever reliable Molly Coddle was again on hand with teapot, steaming urns, jingling cups and a plateful of chocolate biscuits.

Unusually for her though, she was singing merrily in a tuneless but happy mood and her usual teacosy had been replaced with a proper tea lady's hat which she now wore at a jaunty angle.

Sticky and Patrick were attending to the bird table in the middle of the green; luckily the damage was minimal and Patrick was very good at stitching in new pieces of turf that he grew just around the corner on his allotment.

People thought it was strange that he grew grass in his vegetable patch.

Derek retrieved the large 4 x 4 mini tractor from the clubhouse garage and positioned it close to the van as Big Jim collected the large tow-rope from Sticky's trailer.

He fastened one end to the tractor tow bar and then, picking up the other end, stepped back towards the towing loop under the Transit's front bumper.

Derek turned around and fixed his glass eye on Big Jim's back in an unfocused fashion and asking the patently obvious...

'Hurry up, Jim, are you ready yet?'

Molly Coddle leaned out of the club and shouted across the car park...

'Tea up... are you ready for a cuppa?'

Perhaps it was just poor timing, but then of course it wasn't that hard to confuse a hungry Jim at eight o'clock in the morning.

He hadn't had his daily diet of bacon, eggs, sausages, tomatoes, bubble 'n' squeak, mushrooms and beans (well, he was on a diet!) nor had he read his daily paper accompanied by the usual three slices of toast with real butter and fresh strawberry jam!

Jim turned his head this way and that and back again...

'Well....?' said Derek.

'Well... ?' said Molly.

'Er um… yes please,' replied Jim.

In his own mind he had been responding to Molly, but he was regrettably facing Derek at the time and Derek's long-distance sight was never too clever anyway.

He noted that the side of Jim's face that he could see was not covered in hair therefore he MUST be looking his way.

'Here we go…!' shouted Derek and in typical unbridled fashion floored the accelerator.

It was always thought that he should have been a Formula One racing driver, not so much because he would have been any good, just simply that he drove like a madman and it would have been better for all if he had faced one continuous direction.

Had Derek been a little sharper than he was he would have noted that the tractor pulled away a bit too quickly and there wasn't any jolt as it took up the strain of the Transit van's not insubstantial tonnage.

The rope slid quickly through Big Jim's hands and he made a split decision, definitely the right one, on reflection, not to hold on to his end.

The tractor charged merrily across the car park at 15 miles per hour with 10 metres of heavy rope snaking behind it and Rollo in hot pursuit.

It was five minutes later that a rather red-faced Derek trundled back into the car park, having reached the main road junction at the end of the lane before he had realised the 'light load' was a lot lighter than he'd expected and was in fact the vicarage cat hanging onto the tow-rope!

Nine pots of tea, 72 biscuits and two loaves of toasted bread later the grounds began again to resemble the condition they were left in prior to Mr Stubbs, inappropriate rearrangement.

The green had been superbly repaired and if you looked closely you could see that Patrick had actually sewn in the grass with a fine needle and transparent thread just to be on the safe side; meanwhile the uninvited van had been carted off to the police compound along with an equally reticent Mr Stubbs.

The flowerbed had not suffered too badly; a good soaking from the garden hose and some clever work with a stack of bamboo canes ensured that nothing other than a very close inspection would detect that all was not quite as it should be.

It took no more than a few minutes to re-erect the banners the right way up, and with the monumental bird feeding station now a centrepiece in the club's wildlife garden the green was ready at last for the climax of the festival.

The clubhouse was in pristine order; in fact it had never been so spick and span even with the closest attentions from Molly Coddle and her veritable army of dusters, polishes, sprays and disinfectants.

Inside and out blue and white bunting adorned the coving and apex of every wall.

A magnificent flag bearing the club's emblem flapped proudly at the peak of the flag pole.

An impressive array of silver trophies and platters stood in preparation on the top table, burnished until they glittered and dazzled in the early sunlight, and in the centre stood a notice board on which was pinned the life story (with photographs) of the outgoing president, the Rt Hon. Ronald 'Squiffy' Regis.

There was little doubt he cut quite a dashing figure in his RAF blues all those years ago, although nowadays he might have had a little trouble getting his portly figure into the cockpit of a Spitfire.

The history of the club was reflected in picture, certificate, script and press cutting in a multitude of framed presentations across every wall.

Molly Coddle stood at the head of the tea and coffee bar, pristine in a new white apron, with a number of helpers on standby, cleaning and wiping cutlery, teacups and plates.

One or two members were taking the celebrations to extreme lengths, of course, none more so than the green keeper Patrick Albright, who had worked himself into quite a state preparing the bowling surface, and indeed he was at that precise moment out on the green with a comb ensuring that all the grass ran in the right direction.

Inside, several of the members were taking the opportunity to rest for a moment with a cup of tea and to discuss the forthcoming events.

Percy, Big Jim and Tony Havershall were standing by the raffle table which was positively groaning under the weight of all the gifts, some of which were more suitable than others.

There wasn't a square inch of the table that wasn't festooned, cluttered and overflowing with a magnificent array of goods.

They included a dinner service, a whole case of wine, tea towels, boxes and boxes of chocolates, an electric kettle and a toaster, vouchers for luxurious meals, even a weekend break for two in Paris.

Percy wasn't too sure about there being a new copy of the *Kama Sutra* on the table though.

'Well,' said Percy, 'here we are at last.'

'It seems to have taken a long time to get here this year,' reflected Jack.

'It only took me 17 minutes,' said Tony.

Jack looked at him in a quizzical fashion.

'I came on my moped,' continued Tony.

Percy sighed.

Tony, as always, was a little slow on the uptake and understanding of the nature of the conversation.

'Some good prizes for the raffles this year, Percy,' said Jack, with one eye on the stack of chocolate comestibles and the other on the large bottle of fine French brandy.

There was definitely a twinkle of light in his eyes and his mouth was almost drooling in fact.

'I've given myself a good chance this year,' he said and, reaching into his trouser pocket, he pulled out a thick wedge of raffle tickets.

That brought a smile to Percy's face: there were probably enough tickets in Big Jim's hand to win more than a few prizes, but he'd probably paid more for the tickets than the value of the prizes he wanted.

'I've got some too,' said Tony, waving a handful of tickets.

Percy noted that they were a different colour to Jack's.

'How come your tickets are green and Jack's are blue?' he queried.

Tony smiled with a naive and innocent expression.

'Well I bought these last year and didn't win anything so I thought I'd hang on to them and see if I did any better this year.'

'Oh dear,' said Jack and groaned inwardly.

Percy just sighed as per usual; indeed he thought if he was of Native American Indian origin he would probably be known as 'He Who Sighs A Lot.'

Tony put the tickets away and fished a notebook out of his top pocket.

'I've started a book,' he commented, stating what appeared to be the blindingly obvious.

Percy didn't like the way this conversation was heading; he suspected that Tony's writing ability wouldn't suffice to produce anything more complicated than '*NODDY GOES TO TOY TOWN*'.

'Really?' he asked quizzically

Jack was slightly less acidic and decided to offer Tony the benefit of the doubt.

'Er... comedy... thriller... western..?'

'Odds,' said Tony.

Jack was confused and it was patently obvious in his reply:

'Eh?'

Tony reiterated his answer with a little more conviction.

'Odds!'

It was very apparent to him but apparently as clear as mud to the others.

Betting odds,' said an exasperated Tony, 'I'm taking bets on the men's final.'

'Oh,' stated Jack.

'Oh dear,' said Percy, not minding a bit of harmless fun, but not wanting to encourage any gambling or other vices.

Tony continued... He usually did when he was excited about an idea of his and obviously this idea was one that he particularly liked.

'Yes,' said Tony, 'I thought I'd make myself a little bit of beer money and this is a foolproof way to earn a few pounds.'

Big Jim sniggered, really the words 'foolproof ' and 'Tony' didn't go hand in hand, and if there was money involved then he just couldn't imagine that Tony was going to come out on top.

Nevertheless the situation begged that he ask the question.

He gazed up at the notice board to the FINALS DAY listing just to check that Tony was taking bets on players who were actually in the finals.

CLUB FINALS

MEN'S SINGLES

Competitors	Dennis Ditherford vs. Bertie Tattleford
Marker	Derek Dunstable

WOMEN'S SINGLES

Competitors	Sheila Ramsbottom vs. Doris Doolittle
Marker	Cynthia Cobblethwaite
Umpire	Jack Tuttle

TOURNAMENT FINALS

Competitors	Ronald Regis vs. Martin King
Marker	Johnny Jackson

'So you're taking bets on Dennis and Bertie then?' said Jack in a half inquiring, half interested sort of way; after all, if there was money to be made... well?

'Yes,' said Tony, smiling blithely, with a look that seemed to suggest that the lift had not quite reached the top floor yet.

Jack continued the line of inquiry: 'So what odds are you offering on Dennis to win?'

'Well, I'm only going to take a maximum of 50 bets per competitor and fixed bets of £10,' he said, 'that way I won't get caught out by everyone placing bets on one person only.'

He smiled a winning sort of smile and continued, 'And I'm placing odds of 3-1 against for Dennis!'

Jack thought for a while but just couldn't see any fault in Tony's logic; in fact he thought that it seemed quite possible that this was one of those occasions when Tony had actually got something right.

He took the plunge and reached for his wallet.

'Ok,' he said 'I may be making a big mistake but I'll have 10 pounds on Dennis to win,' and with that he fished a 20-pound note out of his wallet.

'Right-o,' smiled Tony, opening his notebook and wetting the tip of his pencil with his tongue.

'Ten pounds on Dennis to win!'

Jack paused in passing over the note as if a sudden thought had occurred to him.

'What odds are you offering on Bertie?'

Tony looked up in the process of writing and smiled...

'Why, 3-1 of course!'

Big Jim groaned in a painful sort of way and took the 20-pound note back.

'Oh dear, heaven protect us,' said Percy and with that patted Jack firmly on the back and walked towards the main door.

He just made it to the other side of the timber before he burst into hysterics.

'Ha! Ha! Ha! Ha! Ha!'

'Oh dearie me, oh God...'

It wasn't often that Percy had reason to chortle, but he was certainly chortling right now and he was clearly having a veritable fit of hysteria.

Percy sat down on the nearest seat as a paroxysm of convulsive laughter gripped him and tears rolled down his face... the club members looked on in total amazement.

* * * *

It was 9.30 a.m. and the clubhouse was a seething hive of activity, the car park was full and even the field behind, which had been generously donated by Squiffy, was full to capacity.

It was a magnificent occasion, to say the least. The local bobby was directing the flow of visitors from the main gate, and nearly all the seats were already occupied with an assortment of club members, guests, bowlers already eliminated from the festival competition, and a large proportion of the local population.

Needless to say, there was a substantial element of the press in attendance, including reporters from the regional newspapers and even one or two of the nationals, although local gazette reporter Jiggy 'Snapper' Jenkins was conspicuous by his absence.

A television van was tucked away in a corner where a film crew were setting up in readiness for the main event.

Percy had a distinct feeling that this would be a bad day for things to go wrong if they were broadcasting a 'live feed' to the nation's news desk.

By the clubhouse there stood a small marquee with comfortable chairs positioned in the shade especially for the prestigious guests who had been invited.

Already several dignitaries from the council, the local Member of Parliament and Mayor had arrived, taken up their seats and were busy exchanging light-hearted banter over cups of Earl Grey.

Also attending were the most senior bowling elite including the county president, Sam 'Iron Man' Harris, and a representative from the English Bowling Association in the form of Cliff Hayward from their publicity department.

It seemed he had managed to pull a few strings and had surprised one and all by turning up with the former world champion, David 'Diddy' Byron.

All in all, this was going to be a day that the club would never forget.

Something caught Percy's eye and he looked over towards the gate where the local policeman was standing stiffly to attention and saluting.

Percy stood up, with his concentration now firmly fixed on the goings-on at the main gate.

A large black limousine pulled slowly through the entrance; it had a pennant flying from its bonnet with a familiar emblem on it.

The vehicle had caught everyone's eye, especially the Rt Hon. Ronald Regis who watched with a mixture of awe, disbelief and amazement.

Apparently the emblem was one he recognised.

Precisely dressed, a chauffeur emerged from the driver's side, stepped quickly round to the rear passenger door, pulled it open and stood smartly to attention.

A very official looking man stepped out into the open; he was a tall, stoutly built, impressive looking gentleman, even more so for the large bushy handlebar moustache that he sported.

He was wearing the full dress uniform of a senior member of the Royal Air Force, and there was no doubt that Squiffy had recognised the pennant of the Air Ministry flying from the staff.

The two men stepped towards each other with huge cheesy grins, arms outstretched in open greeting of old comrades, and their voices cut across the green.

'Squiffy, you old dog, how the hell are you, old chap...?'

'Well, I'll be damned, boomer, you old warmonger, is that you...?'

The men greeted each other with warm bear hugs, a few hearty slaps on each other's backs and a lengthy exchange of friendly ribaldry.

It seemed that the former members of Squiffy's old squadron had also been making a few plans of their own for his retirement and the biggest surprise had just arrived.

Squiffy turned to the other gathered friends, guests and celebrities...

'Ladies and gentlemen, it gives me great pleasure to introduce to you our former Air Marshall, 'Boom Boom' Baker DSO, MBE.'

Percy recognised the name from the photos of Squiffy's military days back in the clubhouse as that of one of his closest friends and colleagues during the war.

Derek seemed to think the name sounded familiar and he remembered Squiffy's 'role play' at the Adventure Park day out.

Percy left the two reacquainted comrades to catch up on the last 30 years and headed back towards the clubhouse.

* * * *

'Ladies and gentlemen, distinguished guests, lords and ladies, members of the press, welcome to the final day of the Lower South-Borough Bowling Festival,' the tannoy system boomed out over the green.

Excitement was at fever pitch and the hushed talk from all of the on-lookers reflected what was to be a fitting culmination to this year's bowling season.

Inside the clubhouse all the finalists were already dressed smartly in their best whites, woods were polished and coloured stickers had been issued for the bowlers participating so that the umpire could easily identify each competitor and the watching spectators could also readily analyse the game situation.

Unfortunately Bertie was playing up.

Indeed it didn't take much for him to become antagonistic or over-reactive and usually it was about the silliest things; right now he was getting 'sticky' over stickers.

As far as he was concerned there was no reason why he couldn't play with the perfectly good ones he had already and these were special ones that his friend in America had sent him.

Covering fully half of the bowling surface, the boldly coloured Day-Glo yellow and lurid orange stickers sported the words WALLY WANGA SPONSORS TAMPA BAY ROWDIES in bold black lettering an inch high.

The advertising was clearly legible from the other side of the green and gave the bowls the appearance of sickly spinning tops as they traversed the green.

'No!'

'Absolutely not!'

'I don't care if the Pope comes in here and tells me it's a life and death situation, I am not removing my stickers.'

Bertie could be very stubborn when he wanted to be, and at this moment he was intractable, obstinate, determined, immovable, resolute, recalcitrant, dogged and tenacious.

Bertie Tattleford had dug in.

He was, for some obscure reason, very attached to his American football stickers, and having travelled half-way around the world to get here he wasn't going to tear them off for anyone.

'But…' said Bernard.

'Come on, old chap…' said Douglas.

'Play the game, old boy…' said Ronald.

'They're only stickers, Bertie…' said Clifford.

'It's the rules…' said Charlie.

'No… No… No… No… No!'

Bertie was adamant, arms crossed, foot stamping, he was much like a petulant schoolboy with his favourite conker.

The committee withdrew in confusion and retired to discuss the problem; after all, the clock was ticking and time was running out.

There was much muttering and puttering within the official huddle: 'DISGRACEFUL, mutter, mutter, DISQUALIFY HIM, mutter, putter, OUTRAGEOUS, putter, mutter, NO RESPECT FOR THE GAME, putter, putter...'

Percy had withdrawn from the consternation and confrontation of the clubhouse and gone in search of a pot of tea to calm the situation.

He returned five minutes later with Molly Coddle in tow carrying a tea tray adorned with a number of cups and saucers, a teapot and a plate of her best chocolate biscuits.

Molly fixed a determined eye on Bertie who was still standing to one side in a typical 'throwing the toys out of the pram' pose.

She poured a cup of her finest tea, tucked a chocolate finger in the saucer, thought for a second, added a buttery digestive as well and then walked over to where Bertie stood.

Molly didn't actually walk, she sort of swayed in a slightly voluptuous way, as if she was on a catwalk, and the steam from the freshly poured cup glistened on the front of her white plastic apron in an almost evocative and sensual manner.

Bertie noticed!

He couldn't help but notice as Molly smouldered her way towards him.

Percy had also noticed!

He gulped, reached quickly for his teacup and nearly choked on the half-eaten digestive he was nervously nibbling.

By the time Molly reached Bertie he appeared to be shaking, almost transfixed, mesmerised and seemingly at a loss for words.

Molly handed him the teacup and he slowly took it with a nervous unwrapping of his folded hands.

'Th–th–th-thank you,' he stammered, the teacup rattling in the saucer as if he had seen a ghost.

Percy took one more furtive look at the two figures, knocked back his cuppa in one mouthful and reached for the teapot.

Molly leant against Bertie's arm in a provocative fashion and leant over towards his ear.

The teacup rattled more loudly... Bertie was acutely aware of the warmth and slight pressure of Molly Coddle's rather impressive breasts pressing against him through the layers of plastic, cotton and under-wiring.

Percy muttered a quick prayer under his breath, took his second 'hit' of tea and reached for the teapot again.

Molly whispered a few words in Bertie's ear and paused for effect.

Bertie began to blush slightly.

She looked him firmly in the eyes and then whispered again.

The teaspoon began rattling like a runaway train on a downhill track.

Bertie began to look like he had sat far too close to a roaring log fire for far too long.

With a final pause, Molly picked up the spoon and placed it in the teacup in a provocative gesture, turned around and flounced off toward the door with a distinctive wiggle of her hips, winking an eye at Percy on the way out.

Percy downed cuppa number three in two seconds flat, most of it missing his mouth completely.

Seconds past unnoticed as Bertie stood, jaw open, contemplating Molly's exit, until he reached for his teacup and thoughtfully drank it down, nearly putting the teaspoon up his left nostril without noticing.

He placed the empty teacup on the table, picked up one of his bowls and walked over to the committee members still huddled in heated debate.

'Right then,' he said in a cheerful, audible voice, 'where are these new stickers?' and proceeded to peel off the Tampa Bay Rowdies.

* * * *

The tannoy system crackled and hissed into life with background noises as a number of bowlers, unaware of the microphone being 'live', continued to chat amongst themselves.

'Nice legs, Sheila!'

'You can't go out there in a thong, Squiffy!'

'That's your eighth cup of tea, Reverend!'

'Looks like you've been at the magic mushrooms, Bertie.

Wakey wakey!'

'Sss-s-s-ss-h-h-hhhh!'

The friendly banter was nipped in the bud by a red-faced and embarrassed Clifford before it got too out of hand, although he was sure that most of the onlookers would be paying close attention to Sheila's legs.

He could see the headlines already about binge-drinking clergy and bowlers taking 'herbal remedies'.

The tannoy burst into life.

'We are ready to begin the proceedings, ladies and gentlemen. To open the finals day, please put your hands together and give a big welcome for the Rt Hon. Clifford James Johnson.'

To a tumultuous round of applause the Lower South-Borough captain stepped out of the clubhouse and onto the green.

He was a much respected and well liked councillor, also young, single and rather good looking in a 'traditional Englishman' sort of way; it was rumoured he was given his middle name after the famous British agent 007.

Consequently there were a number of wolf-whistles and cat-calls from the vicinity of the ladies in the audience and, more worryingly for Clifford, a couple of the men as well!

Clifford held his hand in the air in a warm, humble gesture of thanks and signalled for a bit of quiet as he switched on the radio microphone.

'Thank you, thank you, thank you very much, you are most kind...'

'Before we introduce you to the players in today's grand finals, we have one or two matters to attend to. First, and most importantly, let's officially commence the proceedings!'

A rousing cheer ran around the green and a few of the younger members already caught up in the excitement of the day instigated a 'Mexican wave'.

It pulsed around the spectators in a ripple of pleasure, although one or two of the senior members weren't sure what to do or didn't raise their hands until the 'wave' had long past.

Russell Cobblethwaite got carried away and waved his Zimmer frame above his head, nearly decapitating Phillipa Spindleforth and lifting the wig of Diane Ditherford, which came as a surprise to everyone!

Mind you, she did look very nice in her multicoloured curlers and hairnet!

One could be forgiven for forgetting that the cameras were rolling and Diane couldn't possibly have envisaged close-up shots of her unprepared purple rinse making the six o'clock news!

Clifford continued:

'So without further ado I'd like to call on our chairman and past president Bernard 'Batty' Bartrum to bowl the first wood!'

It was a tradition on the opening day and finals day that the chairman would bowl the first cot and first wood...

Bernard emerged from the clubhouse with a king-sized smile, and a large bowl in his hand.

Soaking up the applause, especially from the ladies, he kept one eye open for those who were clapping more enthusiastically than others just in case there were any eligible spinsters about who took his fancy.

Well, he always had been a bit of a ladies' man!

To a cheer from the clubhouse and some encouragement over the tannoy of 'Stick it on the cot, Bernie,' he bent down on one knee, delivered the wood and stood up to watch it trundle majestically in an arc up the green.

Clifford tapped him on the shoulder.

'Er, Bernard, don't you think you should put the cot up first before you bowl your wood?'

There were a few sniggers from the audience; the microphone was still on.

Bernard peered over the top of his spectacles and up the green where the bowl had now trundled to a halt; sure enough there was no cot in sight.

He was absolutely certain that a cot had been placed at the far end of the green during the 'setting up' early that morning.

A rather puzzled and slightly embarrassed Bernard accepted the offer of another cot from Clifford and sent it on its way up the green where the chortling figure of Big Jim placed it on the marker.

Bernard couldn't see what was so funny, but quite a few of the on-lookers at the other end seemed to be convulsed with stifled laughter.

Apparently the press were enjoying the joke because most of the cameras were focused on the small white object in the distance.

He picked up his bowl, which Big Jim had kindly returned, again bent down to deliver the wood and with a firm hand sent it perfectly on its way towards the waiting cot.

Sure that he had sent the bowl on a perfect line and with the ideal weight, he turned away with a big smile, raising one hand in the air and beaming radiantly towards the clubhouse.

Something emerged from the side ditch at the far end without warning!

If Bernard had been watching keenly in the right direction or had the benefit of a camera monitor he might have previously noticed a pair of large pointy ears and a button nose twitching impishly just above the ditch line on the far side.

Rollo was in very high spirits, exuberant, excited, enjoying the full warmth of the summer sun and loving every second of the mischievous mayhem that possessed him that particular morning. He had, in a manner of speaking, a flea up his proverbial bottom.

He scampered across the green in a manic manner, scooted the white cot into the ditch in a playful 'cat and mouse' fashion and disappeared after it, leaving only his bushy tail jerking spasmodically on the green.

As one the spectators burst into laughter with a spontaneous outburst of mirth and merriment that sallied down the green until it reached Bernard's ears.

Bernard turned towards the source of the laughter to witness the sight of his bowl sitting again at the far end of the green and the cot to be nowhere in sight.

He was speechless!

'Looks like the cat's got your tongue, Bernard,' exclaimed the tannoy.

Clifford leant over Bernard's shoulder and whispered in his ear... 'Watch this, old man,' he said.

With that he picked up another spare cot and bowled it up the green towards Bernard's now stationary wood.

As the white ball drew nearer and nearer towards the other end of the green a bushy tail appeared to rise upward out of the far ditch, soon to be joined by a fluffy head topped by two large ears much like Batman.

It was almost within touching distance of Bernard's previously bowled wood when Rollo charged...

He hurtled across the green, collected the white cot and padded it playfully across the grass with his paws...

Cat and 'toy' disappeared into the ditch where the other two already lay. Just his head and whiskers remained visible to the naked eye.

The audience's response was both spontaneous and infectious.

Bernard and Clifford smiled at each other and joined in the peals of laughter rolling around the congregation.

Over in the ditch, even Rollo appeared to be grinning, like a Cheshire cat.

* * * *

Percy had tried to capture Rollo, but an energetic chase through the rose bed had left more than a few unwelcome scratches and the cat had made good his escape through the lupins.

He decided to call it a day whilst he still had a reasonable proportion of his outer skin intact, mindful that Rollo still had to come home at some point for his dinner, and just maybe he wouldn't get the chicken titbits tonight.

Meanwhile back at the clubhouse the opening ceremony continued on track unabated.

Vice chairman Douglas Doolittle was back behind the microphone and the speakers were booming out the long awaited message to the gathering throng.

'And now, ladies and gentlemen, the finals for today will be as follows... on rink two the gentlemen's club singles will be taking place between our current club champion, Dennis Ditherford, and one of our newest members, Bertie Tattleford. The marker and scorekeeper will be Derek Dunstable, our vice captain.'

More excitable members of the public nudged each other in the ribs and exchanged a few suggestive sniggers behind their raised hands; Dennis was known to wind people up with his 'play' on phantom aches, pains and questionable injuries.

Bertie was an unknown factor but there were a lot of unusual rumours flying about, including some gossip about naked natives down in Adventure World.

Derek was altogether another entity entirely: he was nothing short of a canned volcano capable of erupting at the slightest tremor; if he was to be compared with someone who had a chip on his shoulder then he would definitely have the whole frying pan!

The tannoy paused for the information to sink in and continued...

'On rink eight we have the ladies' club singles final between the current ladies' singles champion, Sheila Ramsbottom, and the ladies' captain, Doris Doolittle. The marker and scorekeeper will be Cynthia Cobblethwaite, head of the ladies' committee.'

Members of the press were very keen to support this match and it was fairly obvious that the cameras would be focused closely on Sheila's lengthy assets long after she had finished bowling her woods.

It was already quite apparent to the gathered members of the paparazzi that Sheila would score big time with their readers even without her woods.

There were one or two 'sporty' publications on hand with open chequebooks in the vain hope that she might be encouraged to do without a lot more than her woods!

The tannoy burst into life once more...

'And on rink five the festival of bowls tournament finals this year, playing for a first prize of £5,000, we have the Lower South-Borough president, the Rt Hon. Ronald Regis...'

A huge cheer swept the rank and file of the club members, proud not only to have one of their very own in the festival finals, but also that it was their president in his last years prior to 'stepping down'.

The spokesman continued above the cheering and shouting.

'Who will play the local and county champion and last year's winner, Martin King.'

An equally large cheer ran through some of the other competitors, notably visiting members of Martin's county team and the Lower South-Borough Clay Pigeon and Associate Game Keepers Association.

'Our marker and scorekeeper will be the British Junior Singles Champion, our very own Johnny Jackson.'

The crowd united in a gesture of goodwill with a round of applause for the young champion, and one or two of the younger ladies were overcome with near-fainting, swooning at the sight of Johnny when he emerged from the clubhouse in his best whites and county blazer.

'Umpire for the day, whose decision will be final and absolute, will be our competition secretary, Jack 'Big Jim' Tuttle.'

It was fairly obvious from the excited cheering and hollering that the audience had high anticipation of this game's competitive value and that 'Big Jim' could be sure to add more than a few helpings of comical comments to the proceedings.

All of the participants were more or less now gathered in front of the green, kitted out in their finest 'clobber', woods polished till they glistened in the sun, and waiting for the umpire to check the validity of the bowls under the rules of the game.

Big Jim, in his usual capacity as the best joker in the club, if not the county, had placed stickers on the bottom of Squiffy's woods that bore the legend 'Best Before 1954'.

Meanwhile Douglas, enjoying his five minutes of fame in front of the microphone, resisted the temptation to do his karaoke *pièce de résistance*, a Jimmy Saville impression, and moved on to the final part of the opening proceedings.

'Before we commence the finals today, ladies and gentlemen, we have a special announcement to make...'

A hushed lull fell across the green as the audience listened up.

'We would like to pay tribute to one of the former founders of Lower South-Borough Bowling Club.'

'A man who has been a figurehead, a driving force and an ambassador of the game for the last 50 years!'

'He has been outstanding in his term of office as our president here at the club and it seems a fitting commendation that today, the last day of the competitive season, he appears not only as our president but also as our club representative in the festival finals.'

A ripple of applause from all the club members acknowledged the achievement, given the strength of the competitive field it was a fine accolade indeed to have reached the final day.

'So, ladies and gentlemen, honoured guests, members of the press, without further ado, please can I ask you to put your hands together and give a very special welcome to the president of Lower South-Borough Bowling Club.'

The excitement and emotion were beginning to tell on Douglas's voice; there was a definite tremble in the vibrato and a lump in his throat as he uttered the final words of his speech...

'The Right Honourable Ronald 'Squiffy' Regis!'

As one the entire ensemble burst into a hearty and rapturous round of applause, many rising to their feet in an inspired and deserving tribute, a standing ovation for a truly outstanding man.

The clubhouse door opened and Squiffy stepped out into the limelight...

* * * *

Squiffy of course knew of the preparations; after all, he was the outgoing president and he was expected to play the part so he had waited in the clubhouse whilst the proceedings had commenced and he could hear the voice of Douglas Doolittle in the background amid the cheers and laughter.

He had chortled to himself greatly when he overheard the commentary about Bernard bowling the first wood and the antics of Rollo the cat.

'Poor old Bernard,' he thought; he of course would never do such a thing, such a mistake would make a county president look ridiculous and he had to be mindful of everything he did in public.

The last couple of hours had been reflective, thoughtful and reminiscent for Ronald and there was more than one tear in the corner of his eye as he prepared himself for the main event.

Ronald had brushed his best blue blazer till not a stray hair remained, checked all his badges, polished his 'chain of office' several times, and ensured his club tie was absolutely spotless; after all, it wouldn't do to walk out on to the green with an egg stain on his tie, would it!

He had paid a visit to the barber the day before so his hair and his handlebar moustache were trimmed to perfection.

A trip to the local store earlier in the week had seen the purchase of a new white shirt with a button-down collar, and great care had been taken to remove all the pins: it wouldn't be a good idea to painfully find one in an unexpected place as he bent over to bowl a wood.

Borrowing Molly Coddle's best steam iron he had earlier ensured that all the creases were removed and the shirt now hung pristine and perfect on a coat hanger by his blazer.

A new pair of expensive patent leather bowling shoes in white sat in an open box, nestling in the tissue paper, by his bowling bag.

He stood at the ironing board in deep contemplation with a distant look in his eyes and a gentle smile on his face as he reflected on where the years had gone to and the memories they brought back.

It was perhaps a good job that no ladies were present at that moment as he stood there in only his long elasticated white socks, string vest and orange polka dot boxer shorts.

Happy at last that he had pressed his best white trousers to perfection, he laid them carefully across the ironing board with matched creases, remembering to turn off the iron; after all, he wouldn't want to walk out onto the green with an unusually shaped burn mark on his bottom!

Percy arrived; ever the thoughtful one he had acquired a cup of tea and a digestive for Squiffy just to settle his nerves for the day.

'Thanks, Reverend.'

'My pleasure,' said Percy, 'It's the least I could do.'

They sat quietly for a few minutes as Squiffy supped his tea and nibbled his biscuit, mindful to avoid getting crumbs down his vest, and for a moment time seemed to stand still.

'Well?' said Percy.

'Well...' said Squiffy.

'Are you ready?' enquired Percy.

'I guess I've always been ready, Percy, I just wonder where all the years have gone,' reflected Squiffy with sadness to his voice.

'But at least they've been good ones,' said Percy.

'Very good ones,' agreed Squiffy whimsically.

'Time to go then, old man,' said Percy with a warm smile and a geniality that came from great respect.

'Yes,' agreed Squiffy, 'time to go...'

'Well, I'll leave you to get ready then,' said Percy, and with that he rose and stepped towards the door.

'Percy!' called Squiffy.

Percy turned his head around...

'Yes Ronald?' (Using his first name out of respect for the man he admired).

'Thanks!'

'My pleasure.'

And with that Percy left the building.

Squiffy smiled to himself and pulled himself sharply together with a smile and a positive shrug of his broad shoulders.

'Come on, old man, it's time to face the future, your public awaits you,' he said to himself.

And with that he began to get ready for his big, big day.

He was miles away, and enjoying the crowd's adulation, as he put on his shirt and fastened his tie.

He was already on the green and bowling his first wood as he slipped into his best blazer and put on his chain of office.

He was playing the winning shot in the finals as he took his new shoes out of the protective tissue and fastened then firmly on his feet.

He was reaching for the winner's cheque of £5,000 to massed cheering as he stepped towards the clubhouse door.

His timing was perfection, as always, and he stepped though the opening just as the public address system blared out, '... Regis!'

The crowd went wild...

They clapped and cheered and hollered and wolf-whistled and applauded and screamed with delight.

Ever Rollo joined in with his own special, rather unique, form of caterwauling from the distant lupins.

Squiffy stepped forward and walked out on to the green, one arm raised in appreciation of the tremendous and enthusiastic ovation being attributed to his arrival.

There was no doubt that the Rt Hon. Ronald Regis was in his element and enjoying the rewards so richly deserved at the pinnacle of his career and his life.

He stepped towards the middle of the green where the chairman stood waiting with the men's captain, Clifford Johnson, ladies captain, Doris Doolittle, and the Mayor.

It looked like he was to receive an accolade, he mused as his eyes focused on the engraved silver salver held by Bernard.

He couldn't help but notice that Doris was looking a little surprised; she had one hand covering her mouth and there was a touch of a 'wild eyed' look about her

'How strange,' he thought.

From the corner of his eye he also noticed that some of the bowlers were smiling over-warmly with broad grins beaming across their faces; in fact one or two were finding it difficult not to laugh.

'How peculiar,' he thought.

His walk towards the gathered group in the middle of the green lost some of his momentum as he noticed a few more things.

The level of applause had not reduced in fervour or volume, but actually increased, and there were a number of complimentary remarks interlaced with the ovation which were slightly unusual.

'Well done, Nobby!'

'Squiffy, you handsome devil!'

'Nothing like going out in style, Ronnie!'

'Lovely legs, you old saucepot!'

'Hope you don't do the decorating!'

One or two of the ladies in the audience were blushing furiously and flapping at their faces with little handkerchiefs, although the more brazen ones were reaching for their binoculars and Molly was taking pictures!

He arrived at the presentation party in a state of confusion but, still managing to retain dignity and poise, he greeted his friends...

'Good morning your Worship,' he paid his respects to the Mayor first, as he felt he should.

'Hello Bernard, Clifford, Doris...'

Doris was speechless, Clifford couldn't get his words out due to an outbreak of sniggering which he was trying to stifle without success, and Bernard actually had tears running down his face as he chortled uncontrollably.

Bernard was the first to manage a few words.

'Well done, Squiffy,' he spluttered, 'that's been the best entrance I've ever seen...'

'But I don't understand..?' said Squiffy, clearly confused.

'Yes,' spluttered Clifford, 'your presidential retirement will be one that goes down in the annals of bowling history...'

Squiffy was very, very bewildered and gave Bernard a searching, quizzical look.

Bernard couldn't speak any more so he just pointed at Squiffy in a slight downward direction.

Squiffy looked down...

A large pair of bright orange boxer shorts covered in large black polka dots stared back at him!

'Oh my God!'

Too late he remembered the freshly ironed, newly creased, white bowling trousers he had left absent-mindedly on the ironing board.

The tannoy blared one final time.

'Modelling our new club colours, ladies and gentlemen, our outgoing president - 'Squiffy'!'

The cheering reached monumental proportions as Squiffy received his retirement award from Bernard and turned to face the crowds, the salver held high in the air and the boxers flapping in the light breeze.

A small cry went up from a member of the crowd, which was soon taken up by one and all...

'One more year..!'

'One more year..!'

'One more year..!'

* * * *

Percy sat down to enjoy the day.

He had a good view, a whole pot of freshly brewed tea, a buttered cheese scone, two cherry crumpets AND a fresh slice of Mrs Spindleforth's gateau made with real strawberries and clotted cream.

Clearly all notions of a diet had departed and he was set to enjoy the delights of a good day's bowling entertainment amongst good company and exceedingly good confectionery.

For once Percy was truly content, and even that pesky vicarage cat, whom he loved really, wasn't going to spoil his day.

He need not have worried about Rollo, because the cat was nowhere near his seat, in fact he was indoors and in the kitchen.

It was, of course, just coincidence that Mrs Spindleforth's half-used pot of clotted cream still remained on the kitchen table!

Percy had given much thought to the three matches about to be played on the club green; indeed he was spoilt for choice and he would have loved to have watched all three.

However he had finally opted to watch the men's singles final between the club champion Dennis Ditherford and 'new boy' Bertie Tattleford.

Over the season Percy had developed a bit of a 'soft spot' for Bertie because as the newest member of his congregation it was his duty to ensure that he was accepted warmly into the fold.

Certainly Bertie's arrival in some respects had been like a breath of fresh air, although the outcome of other darker incidents had been more like a hurricane than a breeze.

Nevertheless Percy saw a good side to Bertie's character and he felt that it had been reflected in his progress through the competitions in the face of stiff opposition.

Not only that, Bertie had been instrumental in bringing certain people out of their shells and there was no doubt that one or two formerly priggish, self-satisfied and stand-offish members were no longer as wearing as they used to be.

There was also a certain, bashful, man-wary spinster of the parish who was no longer the shy, naive person she used to be, and Percy detected a definite twinkle in her eyes nowadays.

He had a feeling that Molly Coddle had her sights firmly set on snaring a certain young man who, until recently, had been blissfully unaware of any matrimonial threat to his carefree life and bachelor existence.

A large smile played across Percy's lips.

'It was going to be a very interesting end to the season,' he reflected.

He wondered how Derek would handle the task of being the official marker and scorekeeper for Dennis and Bertie's match today.

Dennis, the unbeaten singles champion for a number of years, had a reputation as a fine bowler, but he was also prone to 'playing' on sudden injuries that always occurred when he fell behind on the scoreboard. He also had a bad habit of playing slowly and asking questions of the 'marker' as to the state of the game virtually after every wood was bowled.

Derek was not the most patient of people and Percy had a feeling that the day would be highly entertaining.

Sitting where he was, Percy could also keep one eye on the games and any event that required the attention of his good friend Jack Tuttle.

'Big Jim' was the official umpire for the day and it would be his job to mediate in any dispute on 'who's holding shot'.

He was also always game for a laugh, even on a serious day such as this, and he was bound to come out with some sharp witticisms and observations.

Percy felt that if he kept his ears open he might pick up some ideas for his Sunday sermons, although he'd probably have to tone them down just a little bit.

He had a somewhat wistful hope that perhaps the club games would finish before the festival finals and that he'd have a chance to catch the end of 'Squiffy's' heroic and valiant struggle against the county champion Martin King.

Percy checked his watch and noted the time, 10.30 a.m., as right on cue the church clock chimed out the half hour in a rich deep tone.

The tannoy crackled into life.

'Ladies and gentlemen, the games are about to commence. Each player will be allowed two trial ends and then it's 'game on'.'

'Good luck and good bowling to every competitor and may the best man and woman win.'

The crackling stopped.

Percy was pleased to see that the bowlers were going to be allowed to play a couple of 'trial' ends, because he knew Bertie and Squiffy in particular would need to bowl a few woods before they settled into the game.

He poured himself a fresh cup of tea, bit into one of the cherry crumpets and settled back to watch the game.

Percy, for once in his life was happy, content and at total peace with the world: nothing could possibly go wrong, could it?

After all, given the past events of the season, what on earth was there that could possibly happen that would shock or surprise him more than the events of the club's big day out?

The umpire had finished shaking hands with all the competitors and was about to leave the green...

He had wished them all well, having passed on a few words of wisdom to settle Bertie's nerves and also made some comments about Sheila's legs which left her blushing furiously.

Whilst respectfully saluting Squiffy before wishing him well, he had proceeded to remove from his jacket pocket a large pair of Union Jack boxer shorts which he said were 'For Squiffy to wear just in case he manages to win,' which brought a few laughs from the on-lookers.

A hush fell over the audience as, with coins spun, and decisions made, the games got under way.

Bertie really didn't take full advantage of his trial ends and his nerves were clearly showing as he put a bit too much 'oomph' into his game.

His first wood nearly hit Derek on the ankle, the third actually succeeded in squashing Derek's big toe as he was busy picking the second wood out of the ditch, and the fourth one didn't actually make it halfway up the green as he over-compensated.

The game got off to a fairly predictable start, unfortunately for Bertie who just couldn't seem to settle into his game, and a supremely confident 'Sticky' raced off to a convincing lead, falling immediately into his stride.

Whatever Bertie managed to do, Dennis did it just that bit better.

If he was able to get a bowl within 12 inches of the cot then Dennis would get one within six.

On one occasion when Bertie had somehow succeeded in placing three within close proximity to the cot Dennis had the 'rub of the green', and with his final delivery 'picked up' the cot trailing it back to his own woods for a count of four shots.

Bertie looked at the scoreboard and sighed.

It stared back at him in an ominous fashion...

Bertie Tattleford 0 - 14 Dennis Ditherford

Bertie simply could not believe that after 75 minutes of play he hadn't even scored a single shot and that 'Sticky' only needed another seven to win the game and the finals.

It was a completely off-the-cuff event on the furthest rink in play that changed the game for Bertie.

The sun was beating down on the green, it was a very, very hot day and the committee had taken the very unusual step of offering the players a five minute break for cold refreshments to be served at the edge of the rink as long as they were all in agreement.

The decision had been unanimous...

Everyone agreed that it was a good idea in keeping with the spirit of the game, and unlikely to affect any flow to the game as nothing else was being changed on the rink or in the order of play.

Bertie had requested permission to leave the green to answer the call of nature and Derek had given consent without needing to check with the umpire, so Bertie had stepped off the green and made his way wearily along the path towards the club house amid muted comments of:

'Hard luck, Bertie.'

'Keep your spirits up, young man.'

'Don't give up, lad.'

and the suchlike.

Bertie glanced across at the other scoreboards as he passed and made some mental comparisons as he did so; on rink five there appeared to be a good tussle under way between Squiffy and the county champion; Martin was just ahead on 10 shots to nine.

On rink eight however it appeared that the youth and strength of the ladies' champion were having a significant effect on their match: the score stood at 17 shots to 10 in favour of Sheila Ramsbottom.

Bertie continued on his way even more crestfallen now that he saw the other matches were at least competitive whilst he faced the frightening realisation that he might be the first club member ever to be 'whitewashed' in a final.

The ignominy loomed like a spectre over his head and he failed to see the warm smile of Molly Cuddle as she opened the clubhouse door for him.

'What's wrong with you, Bertie? You look like you just received your income tax bill,' said Molly.

Bertie looked up at that and smiled back weakly.

'Worse than that,' he said, 'I'm getting thrashed and there's nothing I can do to stop him.'

'It's all going horribly wrong and I haven't even scored yet,' he bewailed.

'Oh I won't say that,' said Molly softly with a twinkle in her eye.

Bertie missed the inference entirely in stepping past her into the clubhouse, and downhearted he headed for the toilets.

The hallway took him past the offices and kitchen area and he inadvertently gazed inward as he passed the open door.

'How strange,' he thought to himself.

He had at first glance taken the mass of hair on the kitchen worktop to be the top of someone's head bent over the table, no doubt in concentration on cake preparation; however there did seem to be an awful lot of hair and some very unusual colours.

Molly watched Bertie's back disappear up the corridor, a thoughtful expression on her face, and decided that she would have to do something rather special to cheer him up and get his attention.

Meanwhile back in the kitchen Rollo was beginning to feel rather full.

Having started with the half pot of clotted cream, he had then, with appetite wetted, moved onto the fish pie, before discovering the tuna mayonnaise and salmon salad sandwiches.

He now sat in a fishy, creamy, disgustingly smelly, clotted mess of hair and food in the half-eaten remains of the fresh cream Victoria sandwich, now minus its cream; in fact he roughly resembled a large hairy lemon meringue pie with legs and ears.

* * * *

Bertie was on his way back.

He had composed himself and was now more resolute, having held a conversation with the mirror whilst answering nature's call and decided that, whatever happened, he was at the very least going to get on to the scoreboard.

As he walked back past rink eight he found himself momentarily distracted.

The score was now 20-17 in favour of Sheila Ramsbottom, but Doris appeared to hold a maximum four shots on the current end, and Sheila, with one wood to play, was debating her options.

'Who's holding ?' she inquired of the marker.

Cynthia gave the woods a close inspection and called back, 'Doris is holding four shots!'

Sheila appeared to make her mind up at that, chosing to try and reduce the deficit in a dramatic fashion, in the knowledge that, if it came off, she might just clinch the game at the same time.

Cynthia's four woods were in a line, two either side of the cot, close together and about 12 inches to the front of it, whilst Sheila's nearest was almost 30 inches behind the cot.

Sheila stepped up to the mat, set her stance, drew back her arm and delivered the wood in a powerful, muscle wrenching, firing shot that took off up the green like a cannon-ball as she let rip with a loud grunt, much like Venus Williams at Wimbledon only much earthier.

The 'marker' promptly left the green at speed, with dexterity unbecoming of her age, whilst sensible spectators at the far end dived for cover in the shrubbery.

Sheila's bowl thundered along the grass almost quickly enough to leave scorch marks on the grass and collided with the others like a meteorite!

C-R-A-S-H-H-H!

Woods were impressively scattered to the four points of the compass in an exaggerated manner.

Three ended up in the ditch, another in the flowerbed, one trundled down the pathway and under the green keeper's shed whilst the delivery shot rocketed upwards over the hedgerow like a runaway Scud missile.

A loud crashing with evident tinkling of glass followed by several screams indicated that it had spectacularly arrived in Squiffy's conservatory where Mrs Spindleforth was resting with a nice cup of lemon tea after spending all morning since 3.00 a.m. baking and preparing cakes, pastries and savouries.

The remains of the cup now had a size five bowl nestling in it!

As the dust settled, the returning spectators noted that only two woods remained on the green, each about four feet from the cot.

Doris and Sheila, having walked up the green in the wake of the last shot, looked at each other and made the obvious decision.

'Umpire!'

Big Jim stirred from the comfort of his deckchair where he had been enjoying the delightful sunshine whilst partaking of some rather special 'flavoured' coffees, and it could be taken that his rather red nose was not totally due to the strength of the summer sun.

He was about to indulge in a rather lavish slice of chocolate gateau when the shout went up.

The other players were still paused on their refreshment break, so all attention became focused on the outcome of rink eight as Big Jim picked up his attaché case of various measuring devices and headed for the remaining woods.

'I hope you only want me to measure these two,' he commented with a sly smile whilst weighing up the position of the other bowls scattered around the grounds.

The Umpire certainly had no intention of running the end tape measure all the way to Squiffy's conservatory.

Scrutinising the woods carefully to ensure that there was no danger of one toppling over and changing the outcome of the game, he then opened his case.

He hummed and ha-ed, then extracted a string measure from the selection and tried to kneel next to the woods, but the tightness of his trousers combined with his expanding girth and all the coffee were not having it!

Big Jim stood up again to one or two titters from the audience and then chose the only obvious option.

'Excuse me ladies,' he said with a wry smile and then, with legs parted and rigid, he bent over from the waist, easily reaching the objects to be measured but placing a not inconsiderable strain on the seat of his trousers.

The ladies, opting for discretion, that being the better part of valour, averted their eyes from the broad scale of Big Jim's large posterior, although Sheila pondered the fact that it did look like a partial eclipse of the moon.

Grunting with exertion Big Jim succeeded in calibrating the distance of the first gap and, standing astride the remaining gap, he breathed in deeply and bent over to do some comparative measuring.

R-R-R-R-I-I-I-I-I-P-P-P!

The thoroughly tested fabric was strong enough to restrain many things but it wasn't really up to the task of restraining Big Jim's ample proportions as it was exerted to a pressure way beyond several ton per square inch.

Like watching the iceberg tear open the hull of the *Titanic* the stitching failed and the seam tore, in an exaggerated, accelerating fashion, from belt loop to crotch leaving Big Jim's bottom available for public viewing.

Cynthia Cobblethwaite fainted dead away; she was prone to doing that when faced with matters of the flesh.

Sheila and Doris, being made of slightly sterner stuff, took it in their stride but found it very hard not to burst into hysterical laughter.

It was quite obvious to anyone standing 'line astern' of Big Jim's bottom that he was indeed wearing a pink frilly thong; apparently he had a fetish for his wife's underwear.

Big Jim finding himself in a bit of a quandary resigned himself to the inevitable and carried on with the measure whilst the two ladies tactfully stood behind him and shielded his assets from prying eyes; after all it would not do to have the umpire's bottom beamed across the nations television screens.

Decision made, Big Jim stood up cautiously, thanking the two ladies quietly under his breath and slightly red around the edges, announced the result.

'The shot is drawn, dead end, no score!'

* * * *

It had been just a few minutes since Bertie left the green to answer nature's call, but he had seen enough to remind him that anything was possible, any situation retrievable, and no match lost until it was won.

Leaving rink eight with the score at 20-17, passing rink five where the tally had advanced to 12-9 in favour of Martin King, Bertie arrived back, deep in thought, to where Dennis was just finishing his liquid refreshment but the scoreboard still read 14 shots to nil.

'Shall we?' said Bertie, stepping sharply on to the green with a renewed bounce in his step.

'Yes, why not...' agreed Dennis, scenting victory, but noticing Bertie's renewed vigour with some concern.

Most of the spectators watching their game and sensing the result had already moved on to watch the outcome of the other two rinks, with only a handful of Bertie's friends remaining to give him encouragement.

Molly stood by the side door watching with fingers crossed, as well as her arms and legs, and anyone noticing her would have thought that she looked incredibly uncomfortable and must be so hot in the long heavy jacket she was wearing.

The next two ends saw the fickle finger of lady luck turn in a different direction and Bertie at last managed to scrape a couple of single shots.

There seemed little doubt that the small success quickly snow-balled a hundred-fold in Bertie's mind and his growing positivity set the tone for the next half hour.

Bertie drew a wood to within an inch of the cot after Dennis had placed all four of his within six inches.

The very next end a forceful shot played with conviction carried the cot away from Dennis's woods to where Bertie had three of his own waiting.

On the following one he then turned Dennis's bowl out and rested his own in its place for a count of two.

Suddenly Dennis was beginning to look over his shoulder at the scoreboard as Bertie's total began to remorselessly creep up on his own.

It increasingly became a very interesting game to watch; it was especially apparent to Derek that Dennis's ailments seemed to be edging back more and more into the game the closer the players' score drew to each other.

At 14-7 Dennis took the first of several breaks to go to the toilet, the bar and his bowls bag for vital necessities.

As the score reached 16-10 he suddenly became afflicted by a dry cough that kept re-occurring every time Bertie was about to bowl his last wood.

An unexpected attack of cramp in his leg somehow delayed Dennis at 18-15 when Bertie was holding four shots and Dennis only had one wood left to bowl; he was in a very sticky situation and he began to dither...

He eventually played an indecisive shot with lots of weight.

Unfortunately Dennis didn't have much meat to put behind the shot and he was well known for the fact that the harder he bowled a wood, *pro rata* the less accurate it became.

It was therefore no surprise to the on-lookers when the wood left his hand at a reasonable speed and proceeded to loop across rink two in a wide arc before ending up near the ditch next to rink one.

A shout from the on-lookers of 'Drinks all round' clearly indicated the long-standing tradition that followed any bowler seen to be delivering the wood 'against bias' with the consequence that it went the wrong way up the green.

The score now stood in favour of Bertie at 19-18 and there was no doubt that the new man was on a 'high' and riding his luck in good style.

Dennis meanwhile began to complain about discomfort from his old war wounds!

With the ladies' match ended in favour of Sheila Ramsbottom, a number of people had moved down to witness the amazing revival, whilst on the middle rink scores were now tied at 20-20 with both players taking a short breather for refreshments before their final push to the winning line.

As far as 'Sticky' was concerned, the wheels were coming off the wagon in spectacular fashion. He was under pressure and he didn't cope with pressure, no more than a sheet of ice would cope with a Jumbo Jet landing on it; he was beginning to crack.

Six bowls later the cracks resembled large fissures as his first three woods ended up just short of the ditch whilst Bertie's were eight feet away and all very close to the cot; so close in fact Dennis could hardly see it.

Once Bertie had played his final bowl Dennis couldn't see the cot at all; in fact it seemed like the Berlin Wall had been placed in front of it.

'Sticky' picked up his last wood and called down to the marker.

'Where's the cot?'

Derek refrained from his usual jovial comment of 'up this end' and instead indicated the position of the white ball with his left hand, much to the relief of the umpire.

'Sticky' called out again...

'How's my length?'

One or two of the ladies tittered behind him and poked each other in the ribs.

Derek was finding it increasingly difficult to restrain himself but nevertheless he curbed his normally impromptu response and returned the information required.

'You are about eight feet past the cot!'

There was little doubt in Dennis's mind that he was in deep, deep trouble: Bertie was holding more than enough shots for the game. But he dug deep into his long experience and came up with a plan.

What if he could hit Bertie's woods and knock the cot back to his own... he mused to himself. Why that would give him enough shots to win the game... victory would be his!

'Sticky' made his mind up and made his move; for once in his life he combined weight, direction and knowledge in the right proportion and got it right.

His wood careered up the green like a runaway steam engine heading straight towards Bertie's; he couldn't bear to watch so he closed his eyes and waited for the impact as all of the audience drew breath in anticipation.

There was an almighty crash as the bowls collided and ricocheted all over the green; 'Sticky' tentatively opened one eye and looked initially with disbelief and then excitement as he took in the scene before him.

Bertie's four woods were no longer in front of the cot; in fact the cot was nowhere to be seen either and there only remained the three on the green by the ditch where Dennis had first bowled.

'Where's the cot?' shouted Dennis, eager to confirm his monumental victory.

Derek pointed down to the ditch behind the three remaining woods on the edge of the green...

'It's here in the ditch!'

'Sticky' was elated, over the moon, relieved and overwhelmed at the same time and he could not help himself as he rubbed salt in the wound of the crestfallen Bertie.

'And where are my woods?' shouted Dennis, waiting for Derek to indicate the obvious and point out the three remaining on the green.

'They are all in the ditch with the cot!' exclaimed Derek

In the process of throwing his hands in the air in victory Dennis paused...

'S o-r-r-y-y-y, What did you say?'

In total disbelief he threw the challenge contemptuously back down the green, not sure that he had heard Derek correctly.

'Your woods are all in the ditch where you put them,' exclaimed Derek, 'the three remaining on the green are Bertie's!'

'Sticky' groaned deeply to himself; for once luck had not favoured the brave and his perfect shot, played out of desperation, had removed only one of Bertie's woods whilst the other three had shot forward and tapped his own into the ditch!

Dennis turned around to a shell-shocked Bertie, standing open-mouthed with a huge smile on his face as the result sank in...

He had done it!

He had beaten the club champion!

Dennis accepted defeat with a sigh and a graceful, if regretful, relinquishing of his long-held title as he reached out and shook Bertie's hand warmly.

'Well done, lad... well done!'

Bertie would have responded in gentlemanly fashion with a short speech thanking Dennis and Derek and everyone for their support, but events took an unexpected turn and the press were about to get their rich rewards for their patience tenfold.

'Y-e-e-e-e-e-s-s-s-s-s-s!'

A figure charged around the corner in front of Bertie, Dennis, Derek and the gathered entourage, screaming at the top of her voice.

It was a woman, of that they were certain: dressed only in white trainers the female figure could hardly be missed. Lower South-Borough had its very first streaker and the press were loving every second!

Bertie was gob-smacked, beyond comprehension, stumped for words, as he watched the voluptuous, full figured and unmistakeably naked body of Molly Coddle, spinster of the parish, run across the green in full view.

Apparently Page Three was about to get a brand new set of bowling poses.

A large white banner trailed behind Molly, held open by her two outstretched hands and flapping in the breeze. It was easy to read because the other end was weighted down by a large mass acting as ballast.

Covered head to paw in clotted cream, mayonnaise and dried sponge cake, the over-stuffed, over-loaded and over-excited Rollo hung on for dear life in a mixture of exhilaration and desperation.

The vicarage cat had been quietly curled up on a pile of linen just around the corner from the noisy clubhouse, anticipating a fairly lengthy snooze in which to sleep off the effects of his binge-eating and, as per usual, he had no idea whatsoever of the impending aerobic entertainment.

He didn't really fly through the air with the greatest of ease although the press headline of the following day was an absolute cracker; it read 'KITTY KITTY BANG BANG...'

Bertie read the banner as Molly flounced by.

'I LOVE YOU BERTIE TATTLEFORD!' read the inscription in bold black lettering nearly two feet high.

'Looks like you've won two prizes today,' commented Squiffy as he walked past with a scoreboard in hand...

'Club singles and Molly's heart, that's quite an achievement, well done, young lad!'

Bertie looked up from the grass bank where he had sat down rather heavily from the shock, emotion and events just past; he had a very stupid grin of happiness on his face.

'How did you get on?' he asked of Squiffy.

Squiffy looked back with an equally stupid expression as he turned the scoreboard round for all to see.

'21-20 ... I won,' he said, 'last wood!'

The audience went wild...

EPILOGUE

Percy sat on the bench in front of the clubhouse all alone with his thoughts and memories.

It was 9.15 on a Sunday morning, and the day after the climactic finish of the Lower South-Borough bowling season; also the day after the finals day of the Festival of Bowls.

He had arrived back early after his morning service and now sat alone with a cup of Earl Grey enjoying the peace, tranquillity and warmth of the late summer sunshine.

It had been a monumental season and one that had seen a number of changes in his congregation, not just in attendances either.

There was a real and genuine feeling of camaraderie and fellowship of the spirit within the club, and he could be assured that there would be plenty more adventures for them all when they went indoors for the winter season.

The previous day had been amazing, astounding, nerve racking and just the best bowls festival ever!

There had been moments of outrageous comedy and amusing misfortune amid some brilliant gamesmanship.

Bertie Tattleford's success in the club singles had become a talking point that would be a coffee conversation piece for years to come.

So would Molly's proposal of marriage!

Rollo had not been in the best of health after his impromptu hang-gliding demonstration and had retired at great speed, on landing, to the safety of the rose bed.

It would appear his intention was to divest himself of the digested, or rather undigested, contents of the kitchen raid.

He had discovered too late that fresh cream and strawberry jam did not mix too well with fish pie and smoked salmon.

It was perhaps a trifle unfortunate that Jiggy Jenkins, who had 'snuck in' with his camera, was hiding *in flagrante* in the flowerbed when Rollo arrived.

Well, we'll leave the rest to your imagination, but Jiggy definitely needed a long bath and a lot of soap!

Bertie and Molly had 'disappeared' overnight and the rumour was that they had taken a 'spur of the moment' Caribbean holiday that involved a lot of sparsely inhabited desert islands and a sailing yacht.

Squiffy's triumph at the festival in his last presidential year after 50 glorious years at the helm had been a fitting climax and tribute both to the club and to him.

The radiant smile on his face as he lifted the trophy and received his winnings was the idyllic picture of 'nirvana found'.

The perfect gentleman had the most perfect day and yes, of course, he left behind the memory of other great achievements as well, namely that of revealing his boxer shorts to the world!

Percy had a feeling that just maybe Squiffy might come back next year in an 'honorary' capacity.

Reflecting on his own position in life, Percy also had some hard decisions to make following his offer from the bishop to take up the position of religious representative of the faith for eastern England.

The position entailed a year's sabbatical overseas including a trip to Rome, just to see 'how the other half did it' as his bishop had commented.

After all, the opportunity to work in the same neighbourhood as the Pope was a chance of a lifetime.

Percy was in a quandary and life was still full of unexpected surprises.

He sighed with a wry smile and then with a last 'slurp' of his tea turned his attention to the final task of his year.

Ahead of him, sitting on the top of the grass bank in all its antique glory sat the 'Beast of South-Borough'.

The Victorian monstrosity which stood for the club's nearest tribute to modern technology in grass cutting, awaited his loving attention.

Its massive tonnage of nuts, bolts, springs and finely adjusted cutting blades made it look like a combine harvester with teeth!

In front a large cutting box more the size of a five-ton rubbish skip bore little paint and many indentations.

To all intents and purposes it looked like somebody had taken a V6 engine, stripped off the cowling and sat it on top of the main assembly.

Added to this some monster truck rollers and a massive reinforced steel handle that would have towed a truck quite happily, the 'Beast' certainly lived up to its reputation.

Percy had for many months avoided having to use the machine, but with Patrick 'Postie' Albright on holiday also, it fell to him to attend to the final cut of the season.

'Oh well,' sighed Percy, 'let's get on with it.'

He muttered a few appropriate words under his breath.

'Into the valley of death rode the six hundred...' Well it seemed appropriate somehow!

Rollo thought so too from his hiding place in the shrubbery.

Percy approached the glistening, well oiled machinery, pulled the dog-eared instruction book from his overall pocket and began checking through the ignition process one step at a time.

He primed the pump with the first tablespoonful of petrol; he could have sworn that the machine actually smiled in anticipation.

With a tentative touch he nudged the choke lever open to its lowest starting position and reached for the starting handle.

Percy began to crank the engine.

The machine eyed him with its steel blades and gave a little shudder, before spluttering easily into life on the very first turn.

PUTT...! PUTT...! PUTT...!

The 'Beast of South-Borough' purred into life like a new-born baby without so much as a shudder or a growl and Percy stood back in astonishment.

'Not so much a beast but a kindergarten child' thought Percy.

He just couldn't believe it!

Taking the bull by the horns, Percy gave the machine a tentative push and it rolled easily, gently towards the wooden ramp that angled from the bank to the bowling green surface 18 inches below.

Rollo watched with mounting excitement and his tail twitched in intense anticipation.

He had spend the entire night sharpening his claws on the side of the timber frame; in fact at one point he had rolled on his back and had a go with all four in a furious frenzied attack.

Finally paw-sore but satisfied the manic moggy slunk off to the bushes to wait, leaving one of the main timber struts no more than the thickness of a matchstick.

Rollo was about to get his own back for all the trials and tribulations of the season past. He had already used three of his nine lives and wasn't intending to lose any more.

Percy, with a happy smile moved the machine forward onto the timber slope in a relaxed fashion, almost dreamlike as he forgot about the day's work ahead and thought about his holidays.

He got as far as the airport in his imagination…

C-R-A-C-K!

The laws of physics and gravity took effect in a fairly disastrous fashion; the ramp gave way with spectacular effect and the heavyweight mechanical dinosaur crashed through and dropped fully to the green.

Percy, taken completely by surprise, hung on for dear life as the 'beast' plunged earthwards…

He would have been fine if he had not held on quite so tightly to the two control levers on the handlebar!

As his right hand pulled the clutch open and dropped the machine into high gear, the left closed on the accelerator with unimaginable consequences.

Already moving in a downward direction, the 'Beast of Lower South-Borough' hit full acceleration instantly as its blades hit the ground, biting deeply into the soft turf like a snarling madcap JCB digger with rabies.

Percy did what most people would do at that stage…

A torrent of grass, dirt, wood splinters and grit already rose like the debris from a tornado as the machinery chewed huge chunks out of the green surface.

Percy panicked… and released his fingers off the right lever, the clutch slammed shut, and the drive shaft engaged the massive twin rollers.

V-R-O-O-O-O-O-M-M-M-M!

Two tons of metal, machinery and mower took off across the green at breakneck speed.

Percy hung on for dear life, his body hanging horizontally astern of the mower like a wind sock as he endured a white-knuckle ride for the second time of his life.

Rollo rolled around the rose bed in what can only be described as an outbreak of cat hysteria at the events unfolding before his eyes.

Reverend and machinery careered in spectacular fashion around and around the green in a chaotic riot of patterns, leaving crop circles all over the green.

A small group of elderly players enjoying a quiet end of season 'roll up' on the end rink ran for their lives as the mechanical cabaret ran across their rink, flattening the bowls into the grass as if they were no more than mushrooms.

The carnage continued...

Rollo's ears perked up sharply and his eyes paid very close attention as he noted that the clerical combo had turned sharply and now headed in his direction.

He was sure he was free from danger because of the large embankment but discretion forced him back on to his haunches, legs tensed for a fast exit.

The vicarage cat would have been quite safe had the reverend not attempted one last gasp effort to stop the mower.

Percy threw his entire bodyweight down on to the handlebar in a foolhardy and vain attempt to disengage the rollers from the green's surface.

It didn't occur to him to simply let go of the control levers, but then again his fingers were probably frozen tighter than welding around them due to fright!

The huge cutting box and one roller lifted momentarily off the green, only for a second, but perfectly timed as they finally made impact with one of the surrounding embankments.

Its angle was sufficient for the mower to race up the incline, reach launch speed and take off...

Rollo looked on in absolute horror as 'the vicar with the runaway ticker' and the 'Beast of Lower South-Borough' left the ground, rose into the air like an overloaded cargo carrier and headed in his direction.

An excited, agitated, and terrified Rollo turned to make an exit that was, to say the least, speedy enough to enter the Formula One championships.

Close behind, Percy and mower returned back to ground level with a thunderous crash, dislodging the cutting box, and parting company with a number of nuts and bolts.

They ploughed into the rose bed at high speed, their progress unhindered and acceleration unabated.

The pride and joy of Patrick's greenery proceeded to get a 'short back and sides' and Percy held on in horror as he paid close witness to the horticultural demolition amid a shower of pink petal fragments.

Roses, lupins, delphiniums and primulas disappeared in a gaily coloured riot of confetti as everything in their path fell victim.

Rollo, running for his life, dug in with his back paws and leapt high into the air over the top of the privet hedge surrounding the club grounds.

Percy and the mower simply just ploughed through it.

They emerged the other side with an angry and bewildered blackbird still sitting in its nest which in turn rested on Percy's head.

The cat ran for its life down the dusty track as the mower with Percy, complete with wildlife, followed close behind, spitting out leaves, chip-bark and gravel.

Former president, Ronald 'Squiffy' Regis stared out of his bedroom window in amazement as they disappeared in a cloud of dust…

'Well,' he thought…

'This is Lower South-Borough after all, and anything that could happen, probably will happen!'